"By the time I was ten. [...] among my most treasured possessions. It still is. The pages are yellowed and the cat has eaten the best part of the cover—but the magic is still there." —David J. Ritchie, *Ares Magazine*

"The re-presentation of these original Buck Rogers stories secures for Philip Francis Nowlan the important place he deserves as a shaper of modern science fiction." —Sam Moskowitz

"We prophesy that this story will become more valuable as the years go by. It certainly holds a number of interesting prophecies, many of which, no doubt, will come true. For wealth of science it will be hard to beat for some time to come. It is one of those rare stories that will bear reading and rereading many times."
—Hugo Gernsback

"The quality of Nowlan's written science-fiction was certainly exceptionally high—even ten years ago, when the magazine science-fiction was only starting, the work Phil Nowlan did was of a grade that would have been acceptable and well rated against the much more highly evolved work of today." —John W. Campbell, Jr.

"Although not as well known as Edgar Rice Burroughs or E. E. Smith, Philip Francis Nowlan was probably their equal both as a writer and as an influence on modern science fiction . . . the Anthony Rogers stories stand up quite well even today. Nowlan was a talented writer, and, despite his small output, he is one of the most influential science fiction writers of the Gernsback era."
—Michael M. Levy, *Twentieth-Century Science-Fiction Writers*

". . . surprisingly sober and realistic dramatizations of the impact of advanced technology on guerrilla warfare. Nowlan, going beyond the mere invention of fantastic weapons, reveals a shrewd grasp of how they affect strategy and tactics. ***Armageddon 2419 A.D.*** has to be read critically today; its style is purest pulp, and its racism is patently offensive. Nevertheless, it remains one of the most imaginative works of military science fiction."
—John J. Pierce, *Great Themes of Science Fiction*

I AWOKE TO FIND THE AMERICA
I KNEW A TOTAL WRECK—
TO FIND AMERICANS A HUNTED
RACE IN THEIR OWN LAND

PHILIP FRANCIS NOWLAN

ARMAGEDDON

2419 A.D.

HEATHEN EDITIONS
THEIR BOOKS. OUR WAY.

Published in the good ole United States of America
by Heathen Editions, an imprint of
Heathen Creative
P.O. Box 588
Point Pleasant, WV 25550-0588

Heathen Editions are available at quantity discounts.
For information and more tomfoolery, check us out online:

heatheneditions.com

@heatheneditions
#heathenedition

Armageddon 2419 A.D. first published 1928
The Airlords of Han first published 1929
Heathen Edition published January 25, 2021
Refreshed January 30, 2023

Totally rad cover art by Tithi Luadthong
Book and cover design by Sheridan Cleland
Set in 9pt Droid Serif
Numbers in Compacta
Titles in Eurostile LT Extended

ISBN: 978-1-948316-16-3

FIRST HEATHEN EDITION

CONTENTS

HEATHENRY:
THOUGHTS ON THE TEXT

Like most kids of the 80s, my introduction to Buck Rogers was network reruns of the short-lived television show. But it was too late: I had been introduced to *Star Wars*, so all other sci-fi of the time simply paled in comparison. Buck Rogers was not Luke Skywalker, Twiki no Threepio, so I wasn't interested. Honestly, the goofiness of the show kept me from these original stories for a long time. Surely, the source material had to be just as cheesy as, if not more than, the show, I imagined.

Boy, was I wrong.

Very wrong.

These stories are vicious. Surprisingly so. Both in Nowlan's direct and detailed descriptions of what is essentially guerrilla warfare and his, at times, very un-pc way of describing the Hans. The latter of which was even edited and toned down in versions republished during the second half of the 20th century.

Here, we've opted for Nowlan's original unedited text as it was first published in *Amazing Stories* 93 years ago. Some may find its language jarring. For me, it acts as a barometer, illustrating just how far we've come as a society—and, when viewed through the lens of current events, a stark reminder of how far we've yet to go.

As for the text itself, our only edits consist of ironing out various spelling inconsistencies of Nowlan's invented technologies between the two stories and his sometimes odd and inconsistent use of italics.

Additionally, we've added footnotes for insta-reference, and Afterwords to offer better context of the impact these stories had in their infancy by two individuals who experienced it firsthand: Cele Goldsmith, editor of *Amazing Stories* from 1959 to 1965, provides the Afterword for *Armageddon 2419 A.D.*, and sci-fi author and *Amazing Stories* contributor Sam Moskowitz provides the Afterword for *The Airlords of Han.*

Finally, let's talk about the cover art by Tithi Luadthong. I love it. If you're not familiar with his work, look him up, support him, buy his endlessly inventive stuff. It's fantastic. All of it.

Sheridan Cleland
Co-Heathen
January 2021

Here, once more, is a real scientifiction[1] story plus. It is a story which will make the heart of many readers leap with joy.

We have rarely printed a story in this magazine that for scientific interest, as well as suspense, could hold its own with this particular story. We prophesy that this story will become more valuable as the years go by. It certainly holds a number of interesting prophecies, of which no doubt, many will come true. For wealth of science, it will be hard to beat for some time to come. It is one of those rare stories that will bear reading and re-reading many times.

This story has impressed us so favorably, that we hope the author may be induced to write a sequel to it soon.

Hugo Gernsback
Amazing Stories
August 1928

[1] A term first coined by Gernsback in 1916 to describe science fiction. Then, to one-up himself, he actually coined the phrase "science fiction" in his editorial of the first issue of *Science Wonder Stories*, June 1929.

ARMAGEDDON

2419 A.D.

FOREWORD

Elsewhere I have set down, for whatever interest they have in this, the 25th century, my personal recollections of the 20th century.

Now it occurs to me that my memoirs of the 25th century may have an equal interest 500 years from now—particularly in view of that unique perspective from which I have seen the 25th century, entering it as I did, in one leap across a gap of 492 years.

This statement requires elucidation. There are still many in the world who are not familiar with my unique experience. Five centuries from now there may be many more, especially if civilization is fated to endure any worse convulsions than those which have occurred between 1975 A.D. and the present time.

I should state therefore, that I, Anthony Rogers, am, so far as I know, the only man alive whose normal span of eighty-one years of life has been spread over a period of 573 years. To be precise, I lived the first twenty-nine years of my life between 1898 and 1927; the other fifty-two since 2419. The gap between these two, a period of nearly five hundred years, I spent in a state of suspended animation, free from the ravages of katabolic processes, and without any apparent effect on my physical or mental faculties.

When I began my long sleep, man had just begun his real

conquest of the air in a sudden series of transoceanic flights in airplanes driven by internal combustion motors. He had barely begun to speculate on the possibilities of harnessing subatomic forces, and had made no further practical penetration into the field of ethereal pulsations than the primitive radio and television of that day. The United States of America was the most powerful nation in the world, its political, financial, industrial and scientific influence being supreme; and in the arts also it was rapidly climbing into leadership.

I awoke to find the America I knew a total wreck—to find Americans a hunted race in their own land, hiding in the dense forests that covered the shattered and leveled ruins of their once magnificent cities, desperately preserving, and struggling to develop in their secret retreats, the remnants of their culture and science—and the undying flame of their sturdy independence.

World domination was in the hands of Mongolians and the center of world power lay in inland China, with Americans one of the few races of mankind unsubdued—and it must be admitted in fairness to the truth, not worth the trouble of subduing in the eyes of the Han Airlords who ruled North America as titular tributaries of the Most Magnificent.

For they needed not the forests in which the Americans lived, nor the resources of the vast territories these forests covered. With the perfection to which they had reduced the synthetic production of necessities and luxuries, their remarkable development of scientific processes and mechanical accomplishment of work, they had no economic need for the forests, and no economic desire for the enslaved labor of an unruly race.

They had all they needed for their magnificently luxurious and degraded scheme of civilization, within the walls of the fifteen cities of sparkling glass they had flung skyward on the sites of ancient American centers, into the bowels of the earth underneath them, and with relatively small surrounding areas of agriculture.

Complete domination of the air rendered communication between these centers a matter of ease and safety. Occasional destructive raids on the wastelands were considered all that was necessary to keep the "wild" Americans on the run within the shelter of their forests, and prevent their becoming a menace to the Han civilization.

But nearly three hundred years of easily maintained security, the last century of which had been nearly sterile in scientific, social and economic progress, had softened and devitalized the Hans.

It had likewise developed, beneath the protecting foliage of the forest, the growth of a vigorous new American civilization, remarkable in the mobility and flexibility of its organization, in its conquest of almost insuperable[1] obstacles, in the development and guarding of its industrial and scientific resources, all in anticipation of that "Day of Hope" to which it had been looking forward for generations, when it would be strong enough to burst from the green chrysalis[2] of the forests, soar into the upper air lanes and destroy the yellow incubus.[3]

At the time I awoke, the "Day of Hope" was almost at hand. I shall not attempt to set forth a detailed history of the Second War of Independence, for that has been recorded already by better historians than I am. Instead I shall confine myself largely to the part I was fortunate enough to play in this struggle and in the events leading up to it.

It all resulted from my interest in radioactive gases. During the latter part of 1927 my company, the American Radioactive Gas Corporation, had been keeping me busy investigating reports of unusual phenomena observed in certain abandoned coal mines near the Wyoming Valley, in Pennsylvania.

With two assistants and a complete equipment of scientific instruments, I began the exploration of a deserted working in a mountainous district, where several weeks before, a number of mining engineers had reported traces of carnotite[4] and what they believed to be radioactive gases. Their report was not without foundation, it was apparent from the outset, for in our examination of the upper levels of the mine, our instruments indicated a vigorous radioactivity.

[1] Impossible to overcome.
[2] A moth or butterfly pupa (between larva an adult) enclosed in a cocoon.
[3] Archaic use of the word, meaning nightmare.
[4] A radioactive yellow ore, often found in sedimentary rocks and near petrified trees, consisting of uranium, radium, and vanadium with composition $K_2(UO_2)_2(VO_4)_2 \cdot 3H_2O$.

ends next p.

On the morning of December 15th, we descended to one of the lowest levels. To our surprise, we found no water there. Obviously it had drained off through some break in the strata. We noticed too that the rock in the side walls of the shaft was soft, evidently due to the radioactivity, and pieces crumbled under foot rather easily. We made our way cautiously down the shaft, when suddenly the rotted timbers above us gave way.

I jumped ahead, barely escaping the avalanche of coal and soft rock, but my companions, who were several paces behind me, were buried under it, and undoubtedly met instant death.

I was trapped. Return was impossible. With my electric torch I explored the shaft to its end, but could find no other way out. The air became increasingly difficult to breathe, probably from the rapid accumulation of the radioactive gas. In a little while my senses reeled and I lost consciousness.

When I awoke, there was a cool and refreshing circulation of air in the shaft. I had no thought that I had been unconscious more than a few hours, although it seems that the radioactive gas had kept me in a state of suspended animation for something like 500 years. My awakening, I figured out later, had been due to some shifting of the strata which reopened the shaft and cleared the atmosphere in the working. This must have been the case, for I was able to struggle back up the shaft over a pile of debris, and stagger up the long incline to the mouth of the mine, where an entirely different world, overgrown with a vast forest and no visible sign of human habitation, met my eyes.

I shall pass over the days of mental agony that followed in my attempt to grasp the meaning of it all. There were times when I felt that I was on the verge of insanity. I roamed the unfamiliar forest like a lost soul. Had it not been for the necessity of improvising traps and crude clubs with which to slay my food, I believe I should have gone mad.

Suffice it to say, however, that I survived this psychic crisis. I shall begin my narrative proper with my first contact with Americans of the year 2419 A.D.

FLOATING MEN

My first glimpse of a human being of the 25th century was obtained through a portion of woodland where the trees were thinly scattered, with a dense forest beyond.

I had been wandering along aimlessly, and hopelessly, musing over my strange fate, when I noticed a figure that cautiously backed out of the dense growth across the glade. I was about to call out joyfully, but there was something furtive about the figure that prevented me. The boy's attention (for it seemed to be a lad of fifteen or sixteen) was centered tensely on the heavy growth of trees from which he had just emerged.

He was clad in rather tight-fitting garments entirely of green, and wore a helmet-like cap of the same color. High around his waist he wore a broad, thick belt, which bulked up in the back across the shoulders, into something of the proportions of a knapsack.

As I was taking in these details, there came a vivid flash and heavy detonation, like that of a hand grenade, not far to the left of him. He threw up an arm and staggered a bit in a queer, gliding way; then he recovered himself and slipped cautiously away from the place of the explosion, crouching slightly, and still facing the denser part of the forest. Every few steps he would raise his arm, and point into the forest with something he held in his hand. Wherever he pointed there was a terrific explosion, deeper in among the trees. It came to me then that he was shooting with some form of pistol, though there was neither flash nor detonation from the muzzle of the weapon itself.

After firing several times, he seemed to come to a sudden resolution, and turning in my general direction, leaped—to my amazement sailing through the air between the sparsely scattered trees in such a jump as I had never in my life seen before. That leap must have carried him a full fifty feet, although at the height of his arc, he was not more than ten or twelve feet from the ground.

When he alighted, his foot caught in a projecting root, and he sprawled gently forward. I say "gently" for he did not crash down as I expected him to do. The only thing I could compare it with was a slow-motion cinema, although I had never seen one in which horizontal motions were registered at normal speed and only the vertical movements were slowed down.

Due to my surprise, I suppose my brain did not function with its normal quickness, for I gazed at the prone figure for several seconds before I saw the blood that oozed out from under the tight green cap. Regaining my power of action, I dragged him out of sight back of the big tree. For a few moments I busied myself in an attempt to staunch the flow of blood. The wound was not a deep one. My companion was more dazed than hurt. But what of the pursuers?

I took the weapon from his grasp and examined it hurriedly. It was not unlike the automatic pistol to which I was accustomed, except that it apparently fired with a button instead of a trigger. I inserted several fresh rounds of ammunition into its magazine from my companion's belt, as rapidly as I could, for I soon heard, near us, the suppressed conversation of his pursuers.

There followed a series of explosions round about us, but none very close. They evidently had not spotted our hiding place, and were firing at random.

I waited tensely, balancing the gun in my hand, to accustom myself to its weight and probable throw.

Then I saw a movement in the green foliage of a tree not far away, and the head and face of a man appeared. Like my companion, he was clad entirely in green, which made his figure difficult to distinguish. But his face could be seen clearly. It was an evil face, and had murder in it.

That decided me. I raised the gun and fired. My aim was bad, for there was no kick in the gun, as I had expected, and I hit the trunk of the tree several feet below him. It blew him from his perch like a crumpled bit of paper, and he *floated* down to the ground, like some limp, dead thing, gently lowered by an invisible hand. The tree, its trunk blown apart by the explosion, crashed down.

There followed another series of explosions around us. These guns we were using made no sound in the firing, and my opponents were evidently as much at sea[1] as to my position as I was to theirs. So I made no attempt to reply to their fire, contenting myself with keeping a sharp lookout in their general direction. And patience had its reward.

Very soon I saw a cautious movement in the top of another tree. Exposing myself as little as possible, I aimed carefully at the tree trunk and fired again. A shriek followed the explosion. I heard the tree crash down; then a groan.

There was silence for a while. Then I heard a faint sound of boughs swishing. I shot three times in its direction, pressing the button as rapidly as I could. Branches crashed down where my shells had exploded, but there was no body.

Then I saw one of them. He was starting one of those amazing leaps from the bough of one tree to another, about forty feet away.

I threw up my gun impulsively and fired. By now I had gotten the feel of the weapon, and my aim was good. I hit him. The "bullet" must have penetrated his body and exploded. For one moment I saw him flying through the air. Then the explosion, and he had vanished. He never finished his leap. It was annihilation.

How many more of them there were I don't know. But this must have been too much for them. They used a final round of shells on us, all of which exploded harmlessly, and shortly after I heard them swishing and crashing away from us through the tree tops. Not one of them descended to earth.

[1] In this context: at sea means confused.

ch. ends next p.

Now I had time to give some attention to my companion. She was, I found, a girl, and not a boy. Despite her bulky appearance, due to the peculiar belt strapped around her body high up under the arms, she was very slender, and very pretty.

There was a stream not far away, from which I brought water and bathed her face and wound.

Apparently the mystery of these long leaps, the monkey-like ability to jump from bough to bough, and of the bodies that floated gently down instead of falling, lay in the belt. The thing was some sort of anti-gravity belt that almost balanced the weight of the wearer, thereby tremendously multiplying the propulsive power of the leg muscles, and the lifting power of the arms.

When the girl came to, she regarded me as curiously as I did her, and promptly began to quiz me. Her accent and intonation puzzled me a lot, but nevertheless we were able to understand each other fairly well, except for certain words and phrases. I explained what had happened while she lay unconscious, and she thanked me simply for saving her life.

"You are a strange exchange," she said, eying my clothing quizzically. Evidently she found it mirth[2] provoking by contrast with her own neatly efficient garb. "Don't you understand what I mean by 'exchange?' I mean, ah—let me see—a stranger, somebody from some other gang. What gang do you belong to?" (She pronounced it "gan," with only a suspicion of a nasal sound.)

I laughed. "I'm not a gangster," I said. But she evidently did not understand this word. "I don't belong to any gang," I explained, "and never did. Does everybody belong to a gang nowadays?"

"Naturally," she said, frowning. "If you don't belong to a gang, where and how do you live? Why have you not found and joined a gang? How do you eat? Where do you get your clothing?"

"I've been eating wild game for the past two weeks," I explained, "and this clothing I—er—ah—." I paused, wondering how I could explain that it must be many hundred years old.

In the end I saw I would have to tell my story as well as I could, piecing it together with my assumptions as to what had happened. She listened patiently; incredulously at first, but with more

---

[2] Amusement, especially as expressed in laughter.

confidence as I went on. When I had finished, she sat thinking for a long time.

"That's hard to believe," she said, "but I believe it." She looked me over with frank interest.

"Were you married when you slipped into unconsciousness down in that mine?" she asked me suddenly. I assured her I had never married. "Well, that simplifies matters," she continued. "You see, if you were technically classed as a family man, I could take you back only as an invited exchange and I, being unmarried, and no relation of yours, couldn't do the inviting."

2

THE FOREST GANGS

She gave me a brief outline of the very peculiar social and economic system under which her people lived. At least it seemed very peculiar from my 20th century viewpoint.

I learned with amazement that exactly 492 years had passed over my head as I lay unconscious in the mine.

Wilma, for that was her name, did not profess to be a historian, and so could give me only a sketchy outline of the wars that had been fought, and the manner in which such radical changes had come about. It seemed that another war had followed the First World War, in which nearly all the European nations had banded together to break the financial and industrial power of America. They succeeded in their purpose, though they were beaten, for the war was a terrific one, and left America, like themselves, gasping, bleeding and disorganized, with only the hollow shell of a victory.

This opportunity had been seized by the Russian Soviets, who had made a coalition with the Chinese, to sweep over all Europe and reduce it to a state of chaos.

America, industrially geared to world production and the world trade, collapsed economically, and there ensued a long period of stagnation and desperate attempts at economic reconstruction.

But it was impossible to stave off war with the Mongolians, who by now had subjugated the Russians, and were aiming at a world empire.

In about 2109, it seems, the conflict was finally precipitated. The Mongolians, with overwhelming fleets of great airships, and a science that far outstripped that of crippled America, swept in over the Pacific and Atlantic Coasts, and down from Canada, annihilating American aircraft, armies, and cities with their terrific disintegrator rays. These rays were projected from a machine not unlike a searchlight in appearance, the reflector of which, however, was not material substance, but a complicated balance of interacting electronic forces. This resulted in a terribly destructive beam. Under its influence, material substance melted into "nothingness;" i.e., into electronic vibrations. It destroyed all then known substances, from air to the most dense metals and stone.

They settled down to the establishment of what became known as the Han dynasty in America, as a sort of province in their World Empire.

Those were terrible days for the Americans. They were hunted like wild beasts. Only those survived who finally found refuge in mountains, canyons, and forests. Government was at an end among them. Anarchy prevailed for several generations. Most would have been eager to submit to the Hans, even if it meant slavery. But the Hans did not want them, for they themselves had marvelous machinery and scientific process by which all difficult labor was accomplished.

Ultimately they stopped their active search for, and annihilation of, the widely scattered groups of now savage Americans. So long as they remained hidden in their forests, and did not venture near the great cities the Hans had built, little attention was paid to them.

Then began the building of the new American civilization. Families and individuals gathered together in clans or "gangs" for mutual protection. For nearly a century they lived a nomadic and primitive life, moving from place to place, in desperate fear of the casual and occasional Han air raids, and the terrible disintegrator ray. As the frequency of these raids decreased, they began to stay permanently in given localities, organizing upon lines which in many respects were similar to those of the military households of the Norman feudal barons,[1] except that instead of gathering together in castles, their defense tactics necessitated a certain scattering of living quarters for families and individuals. They lived virtually in the open air, in the forests, in green tents, resorting to camouflage tactics that would conceal their presence from air observers. They dug underground factories and laboratories, that they might better be shielded from the electrical detectors of the Hans. They tapped the radio communication lines of the Hans, with crude instruments at first; better ones later on. They bent every effort toward the redevelopment of science. For many generations they labored as unseen, unknown scholars of the Hans, picking up their knowledge piecemeal, as fast as they were able to.

During the earlier part of this period, there were many deadly wars fought between the various gangs, and occasional courageous but childishly futile attacks upon the Hans, followed by terribly punitive raids.

But as knowledge progressed, the sense of American brotherhood redeveloped. Reciprocal arrangements were made among the gangs over constantly increasing areas. Trade developed to a certain extent, as between one gang and another. But the interchange of knowledge became more important than that of goods, as skill in the handling of synthetic processes developed.

Within the gang, an economy was developed that was a compromise between individual liberty and a military socialism. The right of private property was limited practically to personal possessions, but private privileges were many, and sacredly regarded. Stimulation to achievement lay chiefly in the winning of various kinds of leadership and prerogatives, and only in a very limited degree in the hope of owning anything that might be classified as "wealth," and nothing that might be classified as "resources." Resources of every description, for military safety and efficiency, belonged as a matter of public interest to the community as a whole.

In the meantime, through these many generations, the Hans had developed a luxury economy, and with it the perfection of gilded

[1] The Normans were a people of mixed Frankish and Scandinavian origin who settled in Normandy circa 912 AD and became a dominant military power in western Europe and the Mediterranean in the 11th century.

ch. ends p. 13

vice and degradation. The Americans were regarded as "wild men of the woods." And since they neither needed nor wanted the woods or the wild men, they treated them as beasts, and were conscious of no human brotherhood with them. As time went on, and synthetic processes of producing foods and materials were further developed, less and less ground was needed by the Hans for the purposes of agriculture, and finally, even the working of mines was abandoned when it became cheaper to build up metal from electronic vibrations than to dig them out of the ground.

The Han race, devitalized by its vices and luxuries, with machinery and scientific processes to satisfy its every want, with virtually no necessity of labor, began to assume a defensive attitude toward the Americans.

And quite naturally, the Americans regarded the Hans with a deep, grim hatred. Conscious of individual superiority as men, knowing that latterly they were outstripping the Hans in science and civilization, they longed desperately for the day when they should be powerful enough to rise and annihilate the Yellow Blight that lay over the continent.

At the time of my awakening, the gangs were rather loosely organized, but were considering the establishment of a special military force, whose special business it would be to harry[2] the Hans and bring down their air ships whenever possible without causing general alarm among the Mongolians. This force was destined to become the nucleus of the national force, when the Day of Retribution arrived. But that, however, did not happen for ten years, and is another story.

Wilma told me she was a member of the Wyoming Gang, which claimed the entire Wyoming Valley as its territory, under the leadership of Boss Hart. Her mother and father were dead, and she was unmarried, so she was not a "family member." She lived in a little group of tents known as Camp 17, under a woman Camp Boss, with seven other girls.

Her duties alternated between military or police scouting and factory work. For the two-week period which would end the next day, she had been on "air patrol." This did not mean, as I first

---

[2] Persistently carry out attacks on; harass.

imagined, that she was flying, but rather that she was on the lookout for Han ships over this outlying section of the Wyoming territory, and had spent most of her time perched in the tree tops scanning the skies. Had she seen one she would have fired a "drop flare" several miles off to one side, which would ignite when it was floating vertically toward the earth, so that the direction or point from which it had been fired might not be guessed by the airship and bring a blasting play of the disintegrator ray in her vicinity. Other members of the air patrol would send up rockets on seeing hers, until finally a scout equipped with an ultrophone, which, unlike the ancient radio, operated on the ultronic ethereal vibrations, would pass the warning simultaneously to the headquarters of the Wyoming Gang and other communities within a radius of several hundred miles, not to mention the few American rocket ships that might be in the air, and which instantly would duck to cover either through forest clearings or by flattening down to earth in green fields where their coloring would probably protect them from observation. The favorite American method of propulsion was known as "rocketing." The *rocket* is what I would describe, from my 20th century comprehension of the matter, as an extremely powerful gas blast, atomically produced through the stimulation of chemical action. Scientists of today regard it as a childishly simple reaction, but by that very virtue, most economical and efficient.

But tomorrow, she explained, she would go back to work in the cloth plant, where she would take charge of one of the synthetic processes by which those wonderful substitutes for woven fabrics of wool, cotton and silk are produced. At the end of another two weeks, she would be back on military duty again, perhaps at the same work, or maybe as a "contact guard," on duty where the territory of the Wyomings merged with that of the Delawares, or the "Susquannas" (Susquehannas) or one of the half dozen other "gangs" in that section of the country which I knew as Pennsylvania and New York States.

Wilma cleared up for me the mystery of those flying leaps which she and her assailants had made, and explained in the following manner, how the inertron belt balances weight:

Jumpers were in common use at the time I "awoke," though they

ch. ends next p.

were costly, for at that time inertron had not been produced in very great quantity. They were very useful in the forest. They were belts, strapped high under the arms, containing an amount of inertron adjusted to the wearer's weight and purposes. In effect they made a man weigh as little as he desired; two pounds if he liked.

Floaters are a later development of *jumpers*—rocket motors encased in inertron blocks and strapped to the back in such a way that the wearer floats, when drifting, facing slightly downward. With his motor in operation, he moves like a diver, headforemost, controlling his direction by twisting his body and by movements of his outstretched arms and hands. Ballast weights locked in the front of the belt adjust weight and lift. Some men prefer a few ounces of weight in floating, using a slight motor thrust to overcome this. Others prefer a buoyance balance of a few ounces. The inadvertent dropping of weight is not a serious matter. The motor thrust always can be used to descend. But as an extra precaution, in case the motor should fail, for any reason, there are built into every belt a number of detachable sections, one or more of which can be discarded to balance off any loss in weight.

"But who were your assailants," I asked, "and why were you attacked?"

Her assailants, she told me, were members of an outlaw gang, referred to as "Bad Bloods," a group which for several generations had been under the domination of conscienceless leaders who tried to advance the interests of their clan by tactics which their neighbors had come to regard as unfair, and who in consequence had been virtually boycotted. Their purpose had been to slay her near the Delaware frontier, making it appear that the crime had been committed by Delaware scouts and thus embroil the Delawares and Wyomings in acts of reprisal against each other, or at least cause suspicions.

Fortunately they had not succeeded in surprising her, and she had been successful in dodging them for some two hours before the shooting began, at the moment when I arrived on the scene.

"But we must not stay here talking," Wilma concluded. "I have to take you in, and besides I must report this attack right away. I think we had better slip over to the other side of the mountain.

Whoever is on that post will have a phone, and I can make a direct report. But you'll have to have a belt. Mine alone won't help much against our combined weights, and there's little to be gained by jumping heavy. It's almost as bad as walking."

After a little search, we found one of the men I had killed, who had floated down among the trees some distance away and whose belt was not badly damaged. In detaching it from his body, it nearly got away from me and shot up in the air. Wilma caught it, however, and though it reinforced the lift of her own belt so that she had to hook her knee around a branch to hold herself down, she saved it. I climbed the tree and, with my weight added to hers, we floated down easily.

3

LIFE IN THE 25TH CENTURY

We were delayed in starting for quite a while since I had to acquire a few crude ideas about the technique of using these belts. I had been sitting down, for instance, with the belt strapped about me, enjoying an ease similar to that of a comfortable armchair; when I stood up with a natural exertion of muscular effort, I shot ten feet into the air, with a wild instinctive thrashing of arms and legs that amused Wilma greatly.

But after some practice, I began to get the trick of gaging muscular effort to a minimum of vertical and a maximum of horizontal. The correct form, I found, was in a measure comparable to that of skating. I found, also, that in forest work particularly the arms and hands could be used to great advantage in swinging along from branch to branch, so prolonging leaps almost indefinitely at times.

In going up the side of the mountain, I found that my 20th century muscles did have an advantage, in spite of lack of skill with the belt, and since the slopes were very sharp, and most of our leaps were upward, I could have distanced Wilma easily. But when we crossed the ridge and descended, she outstripped me with her superior technique. Choosing the steepest slopes, she would crouch in the top of a tree, and propel herself outward, literally diving until, with the loss of horizontal momentum, she would assume a more upright position and float downward. In this manner she would sometimes cover as much as a quarter of a mile in a single leap,[1] while I leaped and scrambled clumsily behind, thoroughly enjoying the novel sensation.

Halfway down the mountain, we saw another green-clad figure leap out above the tree tops toward us. The three of us perched on an outcropping of rock from which a view for many miles around could be had, while Wilma hastily explained her adventure and my presence to her fellow guard, whose name was Alan. I learned later that this was the modern form of Helen.

"You want to report by phone then, don't you?" Alan took a compact packet about six inches square from a holster attached to her belt and handed it to Wilma.

So far as I could see, it had no special receiver for the ear. Wilma merely threw back a lid, as though she were opening a book, and began to talk. The voice that came back from the machine was as audible as her own.

She was queried closely as to the attack upon her, and at considerable length as to myself, and I could tell from the tone of that voice that its owner was not prepared to take me at my face value as readily as Wilma had. For that matter, neither was the other girl. I could realize it from the suspicious glances she threw my way, when she thought my attention was elsewhere, and the manner in which her hand hovered constantly near her gun holster.

Wilma was ordered to bring me in at once, and informed that another scout would take her place on the other side of the mountain. So she closed down the lid of the phone and handed it back to Alan, who seemed relieved to see us departing over the tree tops in the direction of the camps.

We had covered perhaps ten miles, in what still seemed to me a surprisingly easy fashion, when Wilma explained, that from here on we would have to keep to the ground. We were nearing the camps, she said, and there was always the possibility that some small Han scoutship, invisible high in the sky, might catch sight of

[1] Someone please invent these belts already.

us through a projectoscope and thus find the general location of the camps.

Wilma took me to the Scout office, which proved to be a small building of irregular shape, conforming to the trees around it, and substantially constructed of green sheet-like material.

I was received by the assistant Scout Boss, who reported my arrival at once to the historical office, and to officials he called the Psycho Boss and the History Boss,[2] who came in a few minutes later. The attitude of all three men was at first polite but skeptical, and Wilma's ardent advocacy seemed to amuse them secretly.

For the next two hours I talked, explained and answered questions. I had to explain, in detail, the manner of my life in the 20th century and my understanding of customs, habits, business, science and the history of that period, and about developments in the centuries that had elapsed. Had I been in a classroom, I would have come through the examination with a very poor mark, for I was unable to give any answer to fully half of their questions. But before long I realized that the majority of these questions were designed as traps. Objects, of whose purpose I knew nothing, were casually handed to me, and I was watched keenly as I handled them.

In the end I could see both amazement and belief begin to show in the faces of my inquisitors, and at last the Historical and Psycho Bosses agreed openly that they could find no flaw in my story or reactions, and that unbelievable as it seemed, my story must be accepted as genuine.

They took me at once to Big Boss Hart. He was a portly man with a "poker face." He would probably have been a successful politician even in the 20th century.

They gave him a brief outline of my story and a report of their examination of me. He made no comment other than to nod his acceptance of it. Then he turned to me.

"How does it feel?" he asked. "Do we look funny to you?"

"A bit strange," I admitted. "But I'm beginning to lose that dazed feeling, though I can see I have an awful lot to learn."

"Maybe we can learn some things from you, too," he said. "So you fought in the First World War. Do you know, we have very little left

[2] Psycho Boss? What a job title!

ch. ends p. 22

in the way of records of the details of that war, that is, the precise conditions under which it was fought, and the tactics employed. We forgot many things during the Han terror, and—well, I think you might have a lot of ideas worth thinking over for our raid masters. By the way, now that you're here, and can't go back to your own century, so to speak, what do you want to do? You're welcome to become one of us. Or perhaps you'd just like to visit with us for a while, and then look around among the other gangs. Maybe you'd like some of the others better. Don't make up your mind now. We'll put you down as an exchange for a while. Let's see. You and Bill Hearn ought to get along well together. He's Camp Boss of Number 34 when he isn't acting as Raid Boss or Scout Boss. There's a vacancy in his camp. Stay with him and think things over as long as you want. As soon as you make up your mind to anything, let me know."

We all shook hands, for that was one custom that had not died out in five hundred years, and I set out with Bill Hearn.

Bill, like all the others, was clad in green. He was a big man. That is, he was about my own height, five feet eleven. This was considerably above the average now, for the race had lost something in stature, it seemed, through the vicissitudes[3] of five centuries. Most of the women were a bit below five feet, and the men only a trifle above this height.

For a period of two weeks Bill was to confine himself to camp duties, so I had a good chance to familiarize myself with the community life. It was not easy. There were so many marvels to absorb. I never ceased to wonder at the strange combination of rustic social life and feverish industrial activity. At least, it was strange to me. For in my experience, industrial development meant crowded cities, tenements, paved streets, profusion of vehicles, noise, hurrying men and women with strained or dull faces, vast structures and ornate public works.

Here, however, was rustic simplicity, apparently isolated families and groups, living in the heart of the forest, with a quarter of a mile or more between households, a total absence of crowds, no means of conveyance other than the belts called jumpers, almost

---

[3] A change of circumstances or fortune, typically one that is unwelcome or unpleasant.

constantly worn by everybody, and an occasional rocket ship, used only for longer journeys, and underground plants or factories that were to my mind more like laboratories and engine rooms; many of them were excavations as deep as mines, with well finished, lighted and comfortable interiors. These people were adepts at camouflage against air observation. Not only would their activity have been unsuspected by an airship passing over the center of the community, but even by an enemy who might happen to drop through the screen of the upper branches to the floor of the forest. The camps, or household structures, were all irregular in shape and of colors that blended with the great trees among which they were hidden.

There were 724 dwellings or "camps" among the Wyomings, located within an area of about fifteen square miles. The total population was 8,688: every man, woman, and child, whether member or "exchange," being listed.

The plants were widely scattered through the territory also. Nowhere was anything like congestion permitted. So far as possible, families and individuals were assigned to living quarters, not too far from the plants or offices in which their work lay.

All able-bodied men and women alternated in two-week periods between military and industrial service, except those who were needed for household work. Since working conditions in the plants and offices were ideal, and everybody thus had plenty of healthy outdoor activity in addition, the population was sturdy and active. Laziness was regarded as nearly the greatest of social offenses. Hard work and general merit were variously rewarded with extra privileges, advancement to positions of authority, and with various items of personal equipment for convenience and luxury.

In leisure moments, I got great enjoyment from sitting outside the dwelling in which I was quartered with Bill Hearn and ten other men, watching the occasional passersby, as with leisurely, but swift movements, they swung up and down the forest trail, rising from the ground in long almost-horizontal leaps, occasionally swinging from one convenient branch overhead to another before "sliding" back to the ground farther on. Normal traveling pace, where these trails were straight enough, was about twenty miles an hour. Such things as automobiles and railroad trains (the memory of them not

ch. ends p. 22

more than a month old in my mind) seemed inexpressibly silly and futile compared with such convenience as these belts or jumpers offered.

Bill suggested that I wander around for several days, from plant to plant, to observe and study what I could. The entire community had been apprised of my coming, my rating as an "exchange" reaching every building and post in the community, by means of ultronic broadcast. Everywhere I was welcomed in an interested and helpful spirit.

I visited the plants where ultronic vibrations were isolated from the ether and through slow processes built up into sub-electronic, electronic, and atomic forms into the two great synthetic elements, ultron and inertron. I learned something, superficially at least, of the processes of combined chemical and mechanical action through which were produced the various forms of synthetic cloth. I watched the manufacture of the machines which were used at locations of construction to produce the various forms of building materials. But I was particularly interested in the munitions plants and the rocket-ship shops.

Ultron is a solid of great molecular density and moderate elasticity, which has the property of being 100 percent conductive to those pulsations known as light, electricity, and heat. Since it is completely permeable to light vibrations, it is therefore *absolutely invisible and non-reflective*. Its magnetic response is almost, but not quite, 100 percent also. It is therefore very heavy under normal conditions but extremely responsive to the *repellor* or anti-gravity rays, such as the Hans use as "legs" for their airships.

Inertron is the second great triumph of American research and experimentation with ultronic forces. It was developed just a few years before my awakening in the abandoned mine. It is a synthetic element, built up, through a complicated heterodyning of ultronic pulsations, from "infra-balanced" sub-ionic forms. It is completely inert to both electric and magnetic forces in all the orders above the ultronic; that is to say, the *sub-electronic*, the *electronic*, the *atomic*, and the *molecular*. In consequence it has a number of amazing and valuable properties. One of these *is the total lack of weight*. Another is a total lack of heat. It has no molecular vibration whatever.

It reflects 100 percent of the heat and light impinging upon it. It does not feel cold to the touch, of course, since it will not absorb the heat of the hand. It is a solid, very dense in molecular structure despite its lack of weight, of great strength and considerable elasticity. It is a perfect shield against the disintegrator rays.

Rocket guns are very simple contrivances so far as the mechanism of launching the bullet is concerned. They are simple light tubes, closed at the rear end, with a trigger-actuated pin for piercing the thin skin at the base of the cartridge. This piercing of the skin starts the chemical and atomic reaction. The entire cartridge leaves the tube under its own power, at a very easy initial velocity, just enough to insure accuracy of aim; so the tube does not have to be of heavy construction. The bullet increases in velocity as it goes. It may be solid or explosive. It may explode on contact or on time, or a combination of these two.

Bill and I talked mostly of weapons, military tactics, and strategy. Strangely enough he had no idea whatever of the possibilities of the barrage, though the tremendous effect of a "curtain of fire" with such high-explosive projectiles as these modern rocket guns used was obvious to me. But the barrage idea, it seemed, has been lost track of completely in the air wars that followed the First World War, and in the peculiar guerilla tactics developed by Americans in the later period of operations from the ground against Han airships, and in the gang wars which, until a few generations ago I learned, had been almost continuous.

"I wonder," said Bill one day, "if we couldn't work up some form of barrage to spring on the Bad Bloods. The Big Boss told me today that he's been in communication with the other gangs, and all are agreed that the Bad Bloods might as well be wiped out for good. That attempt on Wilma Deering's life and their evident desire to make trouble among the gangs, has stirred up every community east of the Alleghenies. The Boss says that none of the others will object if we go after them. So I imagine that before long we will. Now show me again how you worked that business in the Argonne forest. The conditions ought to be pretty much the same."

I went over it with him in detail, and gradually we worked out

ch. ends next p.

a modified plan that would be better adapted to our more powerful weapons, and the use of jumpers.

"It will be easy," Bill exulted. "I'll slide down and talk it over with the Boss tomorrow."

During the first two weeks of my stay with the Wyomings, Wilma Deering and I saw a great deal of each other. I naturally felt a little closer friendship for her, in view of the fact that she was the first human being I saw after waking from my long sleep; her appreciation of my saving her life, though I could not have done otherwise than I did in that matter, and most of all my own appreciation of the fact that she had not found it as difficult as the others to believe my story, operated in the same direction. I could easily imagine my story must have sounded incredible.

It was natural enough too, that she should feel an unusual interest in me. In the first place, I was her personal discovery. In the second, she was a girl of studious and reflective turn of mind. She never got tired of my stories and descriptions of the 20th century.

The others of the community, however, seemed to find our friendship a bit amusing. It seemed that Wilma had a reputation for being cold toward the opposite sex, and so others, not being able to appreciate some of her fine qualities as I did, misinterpreted her attitude, much to their own delight. Wilma and I, however, ignored this as much as we could.

4

A HAN AIR RAID

There was a girl in Wilma's camp named Gerdi Mann, with whom Bill Hearn was desperately in love, and the four of us used to go around a lot together. Gerdi was a distinct type. Whereas Wilma had the usual dark brown hair and hazel eyes that marked nearly every member of the community, Gerdi had red hair, blue eyes and very fair skin. She has been dead many years now, but I remember her vividly because she was a throwback in physical appearance to a certain 20th century type which I have found very rare among modern Americans; also because the four of us were engaged one day in a discussion of this very point, when I obtained my first experience of a Han air raid.

We were sitting high on the side of a hill overlooking the valley that teemed with human activity, invisible beneath its blanket of foliage.

The other three, who knew of the Irish but vaguely and indefinitely, as a race on the other side of the globe, which, like ourselves, had succeeded in maintaining a precarious and fugitive existence in rebellion against the Mongolian domination of the earth, were listening with interest to my theory that Gerdi's ancestors of several hundred years ago must have been Irish. I explained that Gerdi was an Irish type, evidently a throwback, and that her surname might well have been McMann, or McMahan, and still more anciently "mac Mathghamhain." They were interested too in my surmise that "Gerdi" was the same name as that which had been "Gerty" or "Gertrude" in the 20th century.

In the middle of our discussion, we were startled by an alarm rocket that burst high in the air, far to the north, spreading a pall of red smoke that drifted like a cloud. It was followed by others at scattered points in the northern sky.

"A Han raid!" Bill exclaimed in amazement. "The first in seven years!"

"Maybe it's just one of their ships off its course," I ventured.

"No," said Wilma in some agitation. "That would be green rockets. Red means only one thing, Tony. They're sweeping the countryside with their dis-beams. Can you see anything, Bill?"

"We had better get under cover," Gerdi said nervously. "The four of us are bunched here in the open. For all we know they may be twelve miles up, out of sight, yet looking at us with a projecto'."

Bill had been sweeping the horizon hastily with his glass, but apparently saw nothing.

"We had better scatter, at that," he said finally. "It's orders, you know. See!" He pointed to the valley.

Here and there a tiny human figure shot for a moment above the foliage of the treetops.

"That's bad," Wilma commented, as she counted the jumpers. "No less than fifteen people visible, and all clearly radiating from a central point. Do they want to give away our location?"

The standard orders covering air raids were that the population was to scatter individually. There should be no grouping, or even pairing, in view of the destructiveness of the disintegrator rays. Experience of generations had proved that if this were done, and everybody remained hidden beneath the tree screens, the Hans would have to sweep mile after mile of territory, foot by foot, to catch more than a small percentage of the community.

Gerdi, however, refused to leave Bill, and Wilma developed an equal obstinacy against quitting my side. I was inexperienced at this sort of thing, she explained, quite ignoring the fact that she was too; she was only thirteen or fourteen years old at the time of the last air raid.

However, since I could not argue her out of it, we leaped together about a quarter of a mile to the right, while Bill and Gerdi disappeared down the hillside among the trees.

Wilma and I both wanted a point of vantage from which we might overlook the valley and the sky to the north, and we found it near the top of the ridge, where, protected from visibility by thick branches, we could look out between the tree trunks, and get a good view of the valley.

No more rockets went up. Except for a few of those warning red clouds, drifting lazily in a blue sky, there was no visible indication of man's past or present existence anywhere in the sky or on the ground.

Then Wilma gripped my arm and pointed. I saw it; away off in the distance; looking like a phantom dirigible[1] airship, in its coat of low-visibility paint, a bare spectre.

"Seven thousand feet up," Wilma whispered, crouching close to me. "Watch."

The ship was about the same shape as the great dirigibles of the 20th century that I had seen, but without the suspended control car, engines, propellors, rudders or elevating planes. As it loomed rapidly nearer, I saw that it was wider and somewhat flatter than I had supposed.

Now I could see the repellor rays that held the ship aloft, like searchlight beams faintly visible in the bright daylight (and still faintly visible to the human eye at night). Actually, I had been informed by my instructors, there were two rays; the visible one generated by the ship's apparatus, and directed toward the ground as a beam of "carrier" impulses; and the true repellor ray, the complement of the other in one sense, induced by the action of the "carrier" and reacting in a concentrating upward direction from the mass of the earth, becoming successively electronic, atomic and finally molecular, in its nature, according to various ratios of distance between earth mass and "carrier" source, until, in the last analysis, the ship itself actually is supported on an upward

[1] Capable of being steered, guided, or directed.

ch. ends p. 30

rushing column of air, much like a ball continuously supported on a fountain jet.

The raider neared with incredible speed. Its rays were both slanted astern[2] at a sharp angle, so that it slid forward with tremendous momentum.

The ship was operating two disintegrator rays, though only in a casual, intermittent fashion. But whenever they flashed downward with blinding brilliancy, forest, rocks and ground melted instantaneously into nothing, where they played upon them.

When later I inspected the scars left by these rays I found them some five feet deep and thirty feet wide, the exposed surfaces being lava-like in texture, but of a pale, iridescent, greenish hue.

No systematic use of the rays was made by the ship, however, until it reached a point over the center of the valley—the center of the community's activities. There it came to a sudden stop by shooting its repellor beams sharply forward and easing them back gradually to the vertical, holding the ship floating and motionless. Then the work of destruction began systematically.

Back and forth traveled the destroying rays, plowing parallel furrows from hillside to hillside. We gasped in dismay, Wilma and I, as time after time we saw it plow through sections where we knew camps or plants were located.

"This is awful," she moaned, a terrified question in her eyes. "How could they know the location so exactly, Tony? Did you see? They were never in doubt. They stalled at a predetermined spot—and—and it was exactly the right spot."

We did not talk of what might happen if the rays were turned in our direction. We both knew. We would simply disintegrate in a split second into mere scattered electronic vibrations. Strangely enough, it was this self-reliant girl of the 25th century, who clung to me, a relatively primitive man of the 20th, less familiar than she with the thought of this terrifying possibility, for moral support.

We knew that many of our companions must have been whisked into absolute non-existence before our eyes in these few moments. The whole thing paralyzed us into mental and physical immobility for I do not know how long.

[2] Toward the rear.

It couldn't have been long, however, for the rays had not plowed more than thirty of their twenty-foot furrows or so across the valley, when I regained control of myself, and brought Wilma to herself by shaking her roughly.

"How far will this rocket gun shoot, Wilma?" I demanded, drawing my pistol.

"It depends on your rocket, Tony. It will take even the longest range rocket, but you could shoot more accurately from a longer tube. But why? You couldn't penetrate the shell of that ship with rocket force, even if you could reach it."

I fumbled clumsily with my rocket pouch, for I was excited. I had an idea I wanted to try; a "hunch" I called it, forgetting that Wilma could not understand my ancient slang. But finally, with her help, I selected the longest range explosive rocket in my pouch, and fitted it to my pistol.

"It won't carry seven thousand feet, Tony," Wilma objected. But I took aim carefully. It was another thought that I had in my mind. The supporting repellor ray, I had been told, became molecular in character at what was called a logarithmic level of five (below that it was a purely electronic "flow" or pulsation between the source of the "carrier" and the average mass of the earth). Below that level if I could project my explosive bullet into this stream where it began to carry material substance upward, might it not rise with the air column, gathering speed and hitting the ship with enough impact to carry it through the shell? It was worth trying anyhow. Wilma became greatly excited, too, when she grasped the nature of my inspiration.

Feverishly I looked around for some formation of branches against which I could rest the pistol, for I had to aim most carefully. At last I found one. Patiently I sighted on the hulk of the ship far above us, aiming at the far side of it, at such an angle as would, so far as I could estimate, bring my bullet path through the forward repellor beam. At last the sights wavered across the point I sought and I pressed the button gently.

For a moment we gazed breathlessly.

ch. ends p. 30

Suddenly the ship swung bow[3] down, as on a pivot, and swayed like a pendulum. Wilma screamed in her excitement.

"Oh, Tony, you hit it! You hit it! Do it again; bring it down!"

We had only one more rocket of extreme range between us, and we dropped it three times in our excitement in inserting it in my gun. Then, forcing myself to be calm by sheer will power, while Wilma stuffed her little fist into her mouth to keep from shrieking, I sighted carefully again and fired. In a flash, Wilma had grasped the hope that this discovery of mine might lead to the end of the Han domination.

The elapsed time of the rocket's invisible flight seemed an age.

Then we saw the ship falling. It seemed to plunge lazily, but actually it fell with terrific acceleration, turning end over end, its disintegrator rays, out of control, describing vast, wild arcs, and once cutting a gash through the forest less than two hundred feet from where we stood.

The crash with which the heavy craft hit the ground reverberated from the hills—the momentum of eighteen or twenty thousand tons, in a sheer drop of seven thousand feet. A mangled mass of metal, it buried itself in the ground, with poetic justice, in the middle of the smoking, semi-molten field of destruction it had been so deliberately plowing.

The silence, the vacuity[4] of the landscape, was oppressive, as the last echoes died away.

Then far down the hillside, a single figure leaped exultantly above the foliage screen. And in the distance another, and another.

In a moment the sky was punctured by signal rockets. One after another the little red puffs became drifting clouds.

"Scatter! Scatter!" Wilma exclaimed. "In half an hour there'll be an entire Han fleet here from Nu-yok, and another from Bah-flo. They'll get this instantly on their recordographs and location finders. They'll blast the whole valley and the country for miles beyond. Come, Tony. There's no time for the gang to rally. See the signals. We've got to jump. Oh, I'm so proud of you!"

[3] Front end.
[4] Emptiness.

Over the ridge we went, in long leaps toward the east, the country of the Delawares.

From time to time signal rockets puffed in the sky. Most of them were the "red warnings," the "scatter" signals. But from certain of the others, which Wilma identified as Wyoming rockets, she gathered that whoever was in command (we did not know whether the Boss was alive or not) was ordering an ultimate rally toward the south, and so we changed our course.

It was a great pity, I thought, that the clan had not been equipped throughout its membership with ultrophones, but Wilma explained to me, that not enough of these had been built for distribution as yet, although general distribution had been contemplated within a couple of months.

We traveled far before nightfall overtook us, trying only to put as much distance as possible between ourselves and the valley.

When gathering dusk made jumping too dangerous, we sought a comfortable spot beneath the trees, and consumed part of our emergency rations. It was the first time I had tasted the stuff—a highly nutritive synthetic substance called "concentro," which was, however, a bit bitter and unpalatable. But as only a mouthful or so was needed, it did not matter.

Neither of us had a cloak, but we were both thoroughly tired and happy, so we curled up together for warmth. I remember Wilma making some sleepy remark about our mating, as she cuddled up, as though the matter were all settled, and my surprise at my own instant acceptance of the idea, for I had not consciously thought of her that way before. But we both fell asleep at once.

In the morning we found little time for love making. The practical problem facing us was too great. Wilma felt that the Wyoming plan must be to rally in the Susquanna territory, but she had her doubts about the wisdom of this plan. In my elation at my success in bringing down the Han ship, and my newly found interest in my charming companion, who was, from my viewpoint of another century, at once more highly civilized and yet more primitive than myself, I had forgotten the ominous fact that the Han ship I had destroyed must have known the exact location of the Wyoming Works.

ch. ends next p.

This meant, to Wilma's logical mind, either that the Hans had perfected new instruments as yet unknown to us, or that somewhere, among the Wyomings or some other nearby gang, there were traitors so degraded as to commit that unthinkable act of trafficking in information with the Hans. In either contingency, she argued, other Han raids would follow, and since the Susquannas had a highly developed organization and more than usually productive plants, the next raid might be expected to strike them.

But at any rate it was clearly our business to get in touch with the other fugitives as quickly as possible, so in spite of muscles that were sore from the excessive leaping of the day before, we continued on our way.

We traveled for only a couple of hours when we saw a multi-colored rocket in the sky, some ten miles ahead of us.

"Bear to the left, Tony," Wilma said, "and listen for the whistle."

"Why?" I asked.

"Haven't they given you the rocket code yet?" she replied. "That's what the green, followed by yellow and purple means; to concentrate five miles east of the rocket position. You know the rocket position itself might draw a play of disintegrator beams."

It did not take us long to reach the neighborhood of the indicated rallying, though we were now traveling beneath the trees, with but an occasional leap to a top branch to see if any more rocket smoke was floating above. And soon we heard a distant whistle.

We found about half the Gang already there, in a spot where the trees met high above a little stream. The Big Boss and Raid Bosses were busy reorganizing the remnants.

We reported to Boss Hart at once. He was silent, but interested, when he heard our story.

"You two stick close to me," he said, adding grimly, "I'm going back to the valley at once with a hundred picked men, and I'll need you."

5

SETTING THE TRAP

Inside of fifteen minutes we were on our way. A certain amount of caution was sacrificed for the sake of speed, and the men leaped away either across the forest top, or over open spaces of ground, but concentration was forbidden. The Big Boss named the spot on the hillside as the rallying point.

"We'll have to take a chance on being seen, so long as we don't group," he declared, "at least until within five miles of the rallying spot. From then on I want every man to disappear from sight and to travel under cover. And keep your ultrophones open, and tuned on ten-four-seven-six."

Wilma and I had received our battle equipment from the Gear Boss. It consisted of a long-gun, a hand-gun, with a special case of ammunition constructed of inertron, which made the load weigh but a few ounces, and a short sword. This gear we strapped over each other's shoulders, on top of our jumping belts. In addition, we each received an ultrophone, and a light inertron blanket rolled into a cylinder about six inches long by two or three in diameter. This fabric was exceedingly thin and light, but it had considerable warmth, because of the mixture of inertron in its composition.

"This looks like business," Wilma remarked to me with sparkling eyes. (And I might mention a curious thing here. The word "business" had survived from the 20th century American vocabulary, but not with any meaning of "industry" or "trade," for such things being purely community activities were spoken of as "work" and "clearing." Business simply meant fighting, and that was all.)

"Did you bring all this equipment from the valley?" I asked the Gear Boss.

"No," he said. "There was no time to gather anything. All this stuff we cleared from the Susquannas a few hours ago. I was with the Boss on the way down, and he had me jump on ahead and arrange it. But you two had better be moving. He's beckoning you now."

Hart was about to call us on our phones when we looked up. As soon as we did so, he leaped away, waving us to follow closely.

He was a powerful man, and he darted ahead in long, swift, low leaps up the banks of the stream, which followed a fairly straight course at this point. By extending ourselves, however, Wilma and I were able to catch up to him.

As we gradually synchronized our leaps with his, he outlined to us, between the grunts that accompanied each leap, his plan of action.

"We have to start the big business—unh—sooner or later," he said. "And if—unh—the Hans have found any way of locating our positions—unh—it's time to start now, although the Council of Bosses—unh—had intended waiting a few years until enough rocket ships have been—unh—built. But no matter what the sacrifice—unh—we can't afford to let them get us on the run—unh—. We'll set a trap for the yellow devils in the—unh—valley if they come back for their wreckage—unh—and if they don't, we'll go rocketing for some of their liners—unh—on the Nu-yok, Clee-lan, Si-ka-ga course. We can use—unh—that idea of yours of shooting up the repellor—unh—beams. Want you to give us a demonstration."

With further admonition to follow him closely, he increased his pace, and Wilma and I were taxed to our utmost to keep up with him. It was only in ascending the slopes that my tougher muscles overbalanced his greater skill, and I was able to set the pace for him, as I had for Wilma.

We slept in greater comfort that night, under our inertron

blankets, and were off with the dawn, leaping cautiously to the top of the ridge overlooking the valley which Wilma and I had left.

The Boss scanned the sky with his ultroscope, patiently taking some fifteen minutes to the task, and then swung his phone into use, calling the roll and giving the men their instructions.

His first order was for us all to slip our ear and chest discs into permanent position.

These ultrophones were quite different from the one used by Wilma's companion scout the day I saved her from the vicious attack of the bandit Gang. That one was contained entirely in a small pocket case. These, with which we were now equipped, consisted of a pair of ear discs, each a separate and self-contained receiving set. They slipped into little pockets over our ears in the fabric helmets we wore, and shut out virtually all extraneous sounds. The chest discs were likewise self-contained sending sets, strapped to the chest a few inches below the neck and actuated by the vibrations from the vocal cords through the body tissues. The total range of these sets was about eighteen miles. Reception was remarkably clear, quite free from the static that so marked the 20th century radios, and of a strength in direct proportion to the distance of the speaker.

The Boss' set was triple powered, so that his orders would cut in on any local conversations, which were indulged in, however, with great restraint, and only for the purpose of maintaining contacts.

I marveled at the efficiency of this modern method of battle communication in contrast to the clumsy signaling devices of more ancient times; and also at other military contrasts in which the 20th and 25th century methods were the reverse of each other in efficiency. These modern Americans, for instance, knew little of hand to hand fighting, and nothing, naturally, of trench warfare. Of barrages they were quite ignorant, although they possessed weapons of terrific power. And until my recent flash of inspiration, no one among them, apparently, had ever thought of the scheme of shooting a rocket into a repellor beam and letting the beam itself hurl it upward into the most vital part of the Han ship.

Hart patiently placed his men, first giving his instructions to

ch. ends p. 36

the campmasters, and then remaining silent, while they placed
the individuals.

In the end, the hundred men were ringed about the valley, on
the hillsides and tops, each in a position from which he had a good
view of the wreckage of the Han ship. But not a man had come in
view, so far as I could see, in the whole process.

The Boss explained to me that it was his idea that he, Wilma,
and I should investigate the wreck. If Han ships should appear in
the sky, we would leap for the hillsides.

I suggested to him to have the men set up their long-guns trained
on an imaginary circle surrounding the wreck. He busied himself
with this after the three of us leaped down to the Han ship, serving
as a target himself, while he called on the men individually to aim
their pieces and lock them in position.

In the meantime, Wilma and I climbed into the wreckage, but
did not find much. Practically all of the instruments and machinery
had been twisted out of all recognizable shape, or utterly destroyed
by the ship's disintegrator rays which apparently had continued
to operate in the midst of its warped remains for some moments
after the crash.

It was unpleasant work searching the mangled bodies of the
crew. But it had to be done. The Han clothing, I observed, was quite
different from that of the Americans, and in many respects more
like the garb to which I had been accustomed in the earlier part of
my life. It was made of synthetic fabrics like silks, loose and comfortable trousers of knee length, and sleeveless shirts.

No protection, except that against drafts, was needed, Wilma
explained to me, for the Han cities were entirely enclosed, with
splendid arrangements for ventilation and heating. These arrangements of course were equally adequate in their airships. The Hans,
indeed, had quite a distaste for unshaded daylight, since their light-
ing apparatus diffused a controlled amount of violet rays, making
the unmodified sunlight unnecessary for health, and undesirable
for comfort. Since the Hans did not have the secret of inertron, none
of them wore anti-gravity belts. Yet in spite of the fact that they had
to bear their own full weights at all times, they were physically
far inferior to the Americans, for they lived lives of degenerative

physical inertia, having machinery of every description for the performance of all labor, and convenient conveyances for any movement of more than a few steps.

Even from the twisted wreckage of this ship I could see that seats, chairs, and couches played an extremely important part in their scheme of existence.

But none of the bodies were overweight. They seemed to have been the bodies of men in good health, but muscularly much under-developed. Wilma explained to me that they had mastered the science of gland control, and of course dietetics,[1] to the point where men and women among them not uncommonly reached the age of a hundred years with arteries and general health in splendid condition.

I did not have time to study the ship and its contents as carefully as I would have liked, however. Time pressed, and it was our business to discover some clue to the deadly accuracy with which the ship had spotted the Wyoming Works.

The Boss had hardly finished his arrangements for the ring barrage, when one of the scouts on an eminence to the north, announced the approach of seven Han ships, spread out in a great semi-circle.

Hart leaped for the hillside, calling to us to do likewise, but Wilma and I had raised the flaps of our helmets and switched off our "speakers" for conversation between ourselves, and by the time we discovered what had happened, the ships were clearly visible, so fast were they approaching.

"Jump!" we heard the Boss order, "Deering to the north. Rogers to the east."

But Wilma looked at me meaningly and pointed to where the twisted plates of the ship, projecting from the ground, offered a shelter.

"Too late, Boss," she said. "They'd see us. Besides I think there's something here we ought to look at. It's probably their magnetic graph."

"You're signing your death warrant," Hart warned.

---

[1] The branch of knowledge concerned with the diet and its effects on health, especially with the practical application of a scientific understanding of nutrition.

ch. ends next p.

"We'll risk it," said Wilma and I together.

"Good for you," replied the Boss. "Take command then, Rogers, for the present. Do you all know his voice, boys?"

A chorus of assent rang in our ears, and I began to do some fast thinking as the girl and I ducked into the twisted mass of metal.

"Wilma, hunt for that record," I said, knowing that by the simple process of talking I could keep the entire command continuously informed as to the situation. "On the hillsides, keep your guns trained on the circles and stand by. On the hilltops, how many of you are there? Speak in rotation from Bald Knob around to the east, north, west."

In turn the men called their names. There were twenty of them.

I assigned them by name to cover the various Han ships, numbering the latter from left to right.

"Train your rockets on their repellor rays about three-quarters of the way up, between ships and ground. Aim is more important than elevation. Follow those rays with your aim continuously. Shoot when I tell you, not before. Deering has the record. The Hans probably have not seen us, or at least think there are but two of us in the valley, since they're settling without opening up disintegrators. Any opinions?"

My ear discs remained silent.

"Deering and I remain here until they land and debark. Stand by and keep alert."

Rapidly and easily the largest of the Han ships settled to the earth. Three scouted sharply to the south, rising to a higher level. The others floated motionless about a thousand feet above.

Peeping through a small fissure between two plates, I saw the vast hulk of the ship come to rest full on the line of our prospective ring barrage. A door clanged open a couple of feet from the ground, and one by one the crew emerged.

THE WYOMING MASSACRE

"They're coming out of the ship." I spoke quietly, with my hand over my mouth, for fear they might hear me. "One—two—three—four, five—six—seven—eight—nine. That seems to be all. Who knows how many men a ship like that is likely to carry?"

"About ten, if there are no passengers," replied one of my men, probably one of those on the hillside.

"How are they armed?" I asked.

"Just knives," came the reply. "They never permit hand-rays on the ships. Afraid of accidents. Have a ruling against it."

"Leave them to us then," I said, for I had a hastily formed plan in my mind. "You, on the hillsides, take the ships above. Abandon the ring target. Divide up in training on those repellor rays. You, on the hilltops, all train on the repellors of the ships to the south. Shoot at the word, but not before.

"Wilma, crawl over to your left where you can make a straight leap for the door in that ship. These men are all walking around the wreck in a bunch. When they're on the far side, I'll give the word and you leap through that door in one bound. I'll follow. Maybe we won't be seen. We'll overpower the guard inside, but don't shoot.

We may escape being seen by both this crew and ships above. They can't see over this wreck."

It was so easy that it seemed too good to be true. The Hans who had emerged from the ship walked round the wreckage lazily, talking in guttural tones, keenly interested in the wreck, but quite unsuspicious.

At last they were on the far side. In a moment they would be picking their way into the wreck.

"Wilma, leap!" I almost whispered the order.

The distance between Wilma's hiding place and the door in the side of the Han ship was not more than fifteen feet. She was already crouched with her feet braced against a metal beam. Taking the lift of that wonderful inertron belt into her calculation, she dove headforemost, like a green projectile, through the door. I followed in a split second, more clumsily, but no less speedily, bruising my shoulder painfully, as I ricocheted from the edge of the opening and brought up sliding against the unconscious girl; for she evidently had hit her head against the partition within the ship into which she had crashed.

We had made some noise within the ship. Shuffling footsteps were approaching down a well lit gangway.

"Any signs we have been observed?" I asked my men on the hillsides.

"Not yet," I heard the Boss reply. "Ships overhead still standing. No beams have been broken out. Men on ground absorbed in wreck. Most of them have crawled into it out of sight."

"Good," I said quickly. "Deering hit her head. Knocked out. One or more members of the crew approaching. We're not discovered yet. I'll take care of them. Stand a bit longer, but be ready."

I think my last words must have been heard by the man who was approaching, for he stopped suddenly.

I crouched at the far side of the compartment, motionless. I would not draw my sword if there were only one of them. He would be a weakling, I figured, and I should easily overcome him with my bare hands.

Apparently reassured at the absence of any further sound, a man came around a sort of bulkhead—and I leaped.

I swung my legs up in front of me as I did so, catching him full in the stomach and knocked him cold.

I ran forward along the keel gangway, searching for the control room. I found it well up in the nose of the ship. And it was deserted. What could I do to jam the controls of the ships that would not register on the recording instruments of the other ships? I gazed at the mass of controls. Levers and wheels galore. In the center of the compartment, on a massively braced universal joint mounting, was what I took for the repellor generator. A dial on it glowed and a faint hum came from within its shielding metallic case. But I had no time to study it.

Above all else, I was afraid that some automatic telephone apparatus existed in the room, through which I might be heard on the other ships. The risk of trying to jam the controls was too great. I abandoned the idea and withdrew softly. I would have to take a chance that there was no other member of the crew aboard.

I ran back to the entrance compartment. Wilma still lay where she had slumped down. I heard the voices of the Hans approaching. It was time to act. The next few seconds would tell whether the ships in the air would try or be able to melt us into nothingness. I spoke.

"Are you boys all ready?" I asked, creeping to a position opposite the door and drawing my hand-gun.

Again there was a chorus of assent.

"Then on the count of three, shoot up those repellor rays—all of them—and for God's sake, don't miss." And I counted.

I think my "three" was a bit weak. I know it took all the courage I had to utter it.

For an agonizing instant nothing happened, except that the landing party from the ship strolled into my range of vision.

Then startled, they turned their eyes upward. For an instant they stood frozen with horror at whatever they saw.

One hurled his knife at me. It grazed my cheek. Then a couple of them made a break for the doorway. The rest followed. But I fired pointblank with my hand-gun, pressing the button as fast as I could and aiming at their feet to make sure my explosive rockets would make contact and do their work.

ch. ends p. 44

The detonations of my rockets were deafening. The spot on which the Hans stood flashed into a blinding glare. Then there was nothing there except their torn and mutilated corpses. They had been fairly bunched, and I got them all.

I ran to the door, expecting any instant to be hurled into infinity by the sweep of a disintegrator ray.

Some eighth of a mile away I saw one of the ships crash to earth. A disintegrator ray came into my line of vision, wavered uncertainly for a moment and then began to sweep directly toward the ship in which I stood. But it never reached it. Suddenly, like a light switched off, it shot to one side, and a moment later another vast hulk crashed to earth. I looked out, then stepped out on the ground.

The only Han ships in the sky were two of the scouts to the south which were hanging perpendicularly, and sagging slowly down. The others must have crashed down while I was deafened by the sound of the explosion of my own rockets.

Somebody hit the other repellor ray of one of the two remaining ships and it fell out of sight beyond a hilltop. The other, farther away, drifted down diagonally, its disintegrator ray playing viciously over the ground below it.

I shouted with exultation and relief.

"Take back the command, Boss!" I yelled.

His commands, sending out jumpers in pursuit of the descending ship, rang in my ears, but I paid no attention to them. I leaped back into the compartment of the Han ship and knelt beside my Wilma. Her padded helmet had absorbed much of the blow, I thought; otherwise, her skull might have been fractured.

"Oh, my head!" she groaned, coming to as I lifted her gently in my arms and strode out in the open with her. "We must have won, dearest, did we?"

"We most certainly did," I reassured her. "All but one crashed and that one is drifting down toward the south; we've captured this one we're in intact. There was only one member of the crew aboard when we dove in."

Less than an hour afterward the Big Boss ordered the outfit to tune in ultrophones on three-twenty-three to pick up a translated broadcast of the Han intelligence office in Nu-yok from the

Susquanna station. It was in the form of a public warning and news item, and read as follows:

"This is Public Intelligence Office, Nu-yok, broadcasting warning to navigators of private ships, and news of public interest. The squadron of seven ships, which left Nu-yok this morning to investigate the recent destruction of the GK-984 in the Wyoming Valley, has been destroyed by a series of mysterious explosions similar to those which wrecked the GK-984.

"The phones, viewplates, and all other signaling devices of five of the seven ships ceased operating suddenly at approximately the same moment, about seven-four-nine." (According to the Han system of reckoning time, seven and forty-nine one hundredths after midnight.) "After violent disturbances the location finders went out of operation. Electroactivity registers applied to the territory of the Wyoming Valley remain dead.

"The Intelligence Office has no indication of the kind of disaster which overtook the squadron except certain evidences of explosive phenomena similar to those in the case of the GK-984, which recently went dead while beaming the valley in a systematic effort to wipe out the works and camps of the tribesmen. The Office considers, as obvious, the deduction that the tribesmen have developed a new, and as yet undetermined, technique of attack on airships, and has recommended to the Heaven-Born that immediate and unlimited authority be given the Navigation Intelligence Division to make an investigation of this technique and develop a defense against it.

"In the meantime, it urges that private navigators avoid this territory in particular, and in general hold as closely as possible to the official inter-city routes, which now are being patrolled by the entire force of the Military Office, which is beaming the routes generously to a width of ten miles. The Military Office reports that it is at present considering no retaliatory raids against the tribesmen. With the Navigation Intelligence Division, it holds that unless further evidence of the nature of the disaster is developed in the near future, the public interest will be better served, and at smaller cost of life, by a scientific research than by attempts at retaliation, which may bring destruction on all ships engaging therein.

ch. ends p. 44

So unless further evidence actually is developed, or the Heaven-Born orders to the contrary, the Military will hold to a defensive policy.

"Unofficial intimations from Lo-Tan are to the effect that the Heaven-Council has the matter under consideration.

"The Navigation Intelligence Office permits the broadcast of the following condensation of its detailed observations:

"The squadron proceeded to a position above the Wyoming Valley where the wreck of the GK-984 was known to be, from the record of its location finder before it went dead recently. There the bottom projectoscope relays of all ships registered the wreck of the GK-984. Teleprojectoscope views of the wreck and the bowl of the valley showed no evidence of the presence of tribesmen. Neither ship registers nor base registers showed any indication of electroactivity except from the squadron itself. On orders from the Base Squadron Commander, the LD-248, LK-745 and LG-25 scouted southward at 3,000 feet. The GK-43, GK-981 and GK-220 stood above at 2,500 feet, and the GK-18 landed to permit personal inspection of the wreck by the science committee. The party debarked, leaving one man on board in the control cabin. He set all projectoscopes at universal focus except RB-3," (this meant the third projectoscope from the bow of the ship, on the right-hand side of the lower deck) with which he followed the landing group as it walked around the wreck.

"The first abnormal phenomenon recorded by any of the instruments at Base was that relayed automatically from projectoscope RB-4 of the GK-18, which as the party disappeared from view in back of the wreck, recorded two green missiles of roughly cylindrical shape, projected from the wreckage into the landing compartment of the ship. At such close range these were not clearly defined, owing to the universal focus at which the projectoscope was set. The Base Captain of GK-18 at once ordered the man in the control room to investigate, and saw him leave the control room in compliance with this order. An instant later confused sounds reached the control-room electrophone, such as might be made by a man falling heavily, and footsteps reapproached the control room, a figure entering and leaving the control room hurriedly. The Base

Captain now believes, and the stills of the photorecord support his belief, that this was not the crew member who had been left in the control room. Before the Base Captain could speak to him he left the room, nor was any response given to the attention signal the Captain flashed throughout the ship.

"At this point projectoscope RB-3 of the ship now out of focus control, dimly showed the landing party walking back toward the ship. RB-4 showed it more clearly. Then on both these instruments, a number of blinding explosives in rapid succession were seen and the electrophone relays registered terrific concussions; the ship's electronic apparatus and projectoscopes apparatus went dead.

"Reports of the other ships' Base Observers and Executives, backed by the photorecords, show the explosions as taking place in the midst of the landing party as it returned, evidently unsuspicious, to the ship. Then in rapid succession they indicate that terrific explosions occurred inside and outside the three ships standing above close to their rep-ray generators, and all signals from these ships thereupon went dead.

"Of the three ships scouting to the south, the LD-248 suffered an identical fate, at the same moment. Its records add little to the knowledge of the disaster. But with the LK-745 and the LG-25 it was different.

"The relay instruments of the LK-745 indicated the destruction by an explosion of the rear rep-ray generator, and that the ship hung stern down for a short space, swinging like a pendulum. The forward viewplates and indicators did not cease functioning, but their records are chaotic, except for one projectoscope still, which shows the bowl of the valley, and the GK-981 falling, but no visible evidence of tribesmen. The control-room viewplate is also a chaotic record of the ship's crew tumbling and falling to the rear wall. Then the forward rep-ray generator exploded, and all signals went dead.

"The fate of the LG-25 was somewhat similar, except that this ship hung nose down, and drifted on the wind southward as it slowly descended out of control.

"As its control room was shattered, verbal report from its Action Captain was precluded. The record of the interior rear viewplate shows members of the crew climbing toward the rear rep-ray

ch. ends next p.

generator in an attempt to establish manual control of it, and increase the lift. The projectoscope relays, swinging in wide arcs, recorded little of value except at the ends of their swings. One of these, from a machine which happened to be set in telescopic focus, shows several views of great value in picturing the falls of the other ships, and all of the rear projectoscope records enable the reconstruction in detail of the pendulum and torsional[1] movements of the ship, and its sag toward the earth. But none of the views showing the forest below contain any indication of tribesmen's presence. A final explosion put this ship out of commission at a height of 1,000 feet, and at a point four miles south by east of the center of the valley."

The message ended with a repetition of the warning to other airmen to avoid the valley.

---

[1] Relating to or resulting from torsion (the action of twisting or the state of being twisted).

7

INCREDIBLE TREASON

After receiving this report, and reassurances of support from the Big Bosses of the neighboring Gangs, Hart determined to reestablish the Wyoming Valley community.

A careful survey of the territory showed that it was only the northern sections and slopes that had been "beamed" by the first Han ship.

The synthetic-fabrics plant had been partially wiped out, though the lower levels underground had not been reached by the dis-ray. The forest screen above it, however, had been annihilated, and it was determined to abandon it, after removing all usable machinery and evidences of the processes that might be of interest to the Han scientists, should they return to the valley in the future.

The ammunition plant, and the rocket-ship plant, which had just been about to start operation at the time of the raid, were intact, as were the other important plants.

Hart brought the Camboss up from the Susquanna Works, and laid out new camp locations, scattering them farther to the south, and avoiding ground which had been seared by the Han beams and the immediate locations of the Han wrecks.

During this period, a sharp check was kept upon Han messages,

for the phone plant had been one of the first to be put in operation, and when it became evident that the Hans did not intend any
immediate reprisals, the entire membership of the community was
summoned back, and normal life was resumed.

Wilma and I had been married the day after the destruction of
the ships, and spent this intervening period in a delightful hon-
eymoon, camping high in the mountains. On our return, we had
a camp of our own, of course. We were assigned to location 1017.
And as might be expected, we had a great deal of banter over which
one of us was Camp Boss. The title stood after my name on the Big
Boss' records, and those of the Big Camboss, of course, but Wilma
airily held that this meant nothing at all—and generally succeeded
in making me admit it whenever she chose.

I found myself a full-fledged member of the Gang now, for
I had elected to search no farther for a permanent alliance, much as
I would have liked to familiarize myself with this 25th century
life in other sections of the country. The Wyomings had a high
morale, and had prospered under the rule of Big Boss Hart for many
years. But many of the gangs, I found, were badly organized, lacked
strong hands in authority, and were rife with intrigue. On the whole,
I thought I would be wise to stay with a group which had already
proved its friendliness, and in which I seemed to have prospects of
advancement. Under these modern social and economic conditions,
the kind of individual freedom to which I had been accustomed in
the 20th century was impossible. I would have been as much of
a nonentity in every phase of human relationship by attempting to
avoid alliances, as any man of the 20th century would have been
politically, who aligned himself with no political party.

This entire modern life, it appeared to me, judging from my
ancient viewpoint, was organized along what I called "political"
lines. And in this connection, it amused me to notice how universal
had become the use of the word "boss." The leader, the person in
charge or authority over anything, was a "boss." There was as little
formality in his relations with his followers as there was in the case
of the 20th century political boss, and the same high respect paid
him by his followers as well as the same high consideration by him
of their interests. He was just as much of an autocrat, and just as

much dependent upon the general popularity of his actions for the ability to maintain his autocracy.

The sub-boss who could not command the loyalty of his followers was as quickly deposed, either by them or by his superiors, as the ancient ward leader of the 20th century who lost control of his votes.

As society was organized in the 20th century, I do not believe the system could have worked in anything but politics. I tremble to think what would have happened, had the attempt been made to handle the A. E. F.[1] this way during the First World War, instead of by that rigid military discipline and complete assumption of the individual as a mere standardized cog in the machine.

But owing to the centuries of desperate suffering the people had endured at the hands of the Hans, there developed a spirit of self-sacrifice and consideration for the common good that made the scheme applicable and efficient in all forms of human cooperation.

I have a little heresy about all this, however. My associates regard the thought with as much horror as many worthy people of the 20th century felt in regard to any heretical suggestion that the original outline of government as laid down in the First Constitution did not apply as well to 20th century conditions as to those of the early 19th.

In later years, I felt that there was a certain softening of moral fiber among the people, since the Hans had been finally destroyed with all their works; and Americans have developed a new luxury economy. I have seen signs of the reawakening of greed, of selfishness. The eternal cycle seems to be at work. I fear that slowly, though surely, private wealth is reappearing, codes of inflexibility are developing; they will be followed by corruption, degradation; and in the end some cataclysmic event will end this era and usher in a new one.

All this, however, is wandering afar from my story, which concerns our early battles against the Hans, and not our more modern problems of self-control.

Our victory over the seven Han ships had set the country ablaze. The secret had been carefully communicated to the other gangs,

---

[1] American Expeditionary Forces.

ch. ends p. 50

and the country was agog[2] from one end to the other. There was feverish activity in the ammunition plants, and the hunting of stray Han ships became an enthusiastic sport. The results were disastrous to our hereditary enemies.

From the Pacific Coast came the report of a great transpacific liner of 75,000 tons "lift" being brought to earth from a position of invisibility above the clouds. A dozen Sacramentos had caught the hazy outlines of its rep-rays approaching them, head-on, in the twilight, like ghostly pillars reaching into the sky. They had fired rockets into it with ease, whereas they would have had difficulty in hitting it if it had been moving at right angles to their position. They got one rep-ray. The other was not strong enough to hold it up. It floated to earth, nose down, and since it was unarmed and unarmored, they had no difficulty in shooting it to pieces and massacring its crew and passengers. It seemed barbarous to me. But then I did not have centuries of bitter persecution in my blood.

From the Jersey Beaches we received news of the destruction of a Nu-yok-A-lan-a liner. The Sand-snipers, practically invisible in their sand-colored clothing, and half buried along the beaches, lay in wait for days, risking the play of dis-beams along the route, and finally registering four hits within a week. The Hans discontinued their service along this route, and as evidence that they were badly shaken by our success, sent no raiders down the Beaches.

It was a few weeks later that Big Boss Hart sent for me.

"Tony," he said, "There are two things I want to talk to you about. One of them will become public property in a few days, I think. We aren't going to get any more Han ships by shooting up their repellor rays unless we use much larger rockets. They are wise to us now. They're putting armor of great thickness in the hulls of their ships below the rep-ray machines. Near Bah-flo this morning a party of Eries shot one without success. The explosions staggered her, but did not penetrate. As near as we can gather from their reports, their laboratories have developed a new alloy of great tensile strength and elasticity which nevertheless lets the rep-rays through like a sieve. Our reports indicate that the Eries' rockets bounced off

---

[2] Very eager or curious to hear or see something.

harmlessly. Most of the party was wiped out as the dis-rays went into action on them.

"This is going to mean real business for all of the gangs before long. The Big Bosses have just held a national ultrophone council. It was decided that America must organize on a national basis. The first move is to develop sectional organization by Zones. I have been made Superboss of the Mid-Atlantic Zone.

"We're in for it now. The Hans are sure to launch reprisal expeditions. If we're to save the race we must keep them away from our camps and plants. I'm thinking of developing a permanent field force, along the lines of the regular armies of the 20th century you told me about. Its business will be twofold: to carry the warfare as much as possible to the Hans, and to serve as a decoy, to keep their attention from our plants. I'm going to need your help in this.

"The other thing I wanted to talk to you about is this: amazing and impossible as it seems, there is a group, or perhaps an entire gang, somewhere among us, that is betraying us to the Hans. It may be the Bad Bloods, or it may be one of those gangs who live near one of the Han cities. You know, a hundred and fifteen or twenty years ago there were certain of these people's ancestors who actually degraded themselves by mating with the Hans, sometimes even serving them as slaves, in the days before they brought all their service machinery to perfection.

"There is such a gang, called the Nagras, up near Bah-flo, and another in Mid-Jersey that men call the Pineys. But I hardly suspect the Pineys. There is little intelligence among them. They wouldn't have the information to give the Hans, nor would they be capable of imparting it. They're absolute savages."

"Just what evidence is there that anybody has been clearing information to the Hans?" I asked.

"Well," he replied, "first of all there was that raid upon us. That first Han ship knew the location of our plants exactly. You remember it floated directly into position above the valley and began a systematic beaming. Then, the Hans quite obviously have learned that we are picking up their electrophone waves, for they've gone back to their old, but extremely accurate, system of directional control. But we've been getting them for the past week by installing

ch. ends next p.

automatic re-broadcast units along the scar paths. This is what the Americans called those strips of country directly under the regular ship routes of the Hans, who as a matter of precaution frequently blasted them with their dis beams to prevent the growth of foliage which might give shelter to the Americans. But they've been beaming those paths so hard, it looks as though they even had information of this strategy. And in addition, they've been using code. Finally, we've picked up three of their messages in which they discuss, with some nervousness, the existence of our 'mysterious' ultrophone."

"But they still have no knowledge of the nature and control of ultronic activity?" I asked.

"No," said the Big Boss thoughtfully, "they don't seem to have a bit of information about it."

"Then it's quite clear," I ventured, "that whoever is 'clearing' us to them is doing it piecemeal. It sounds like a bit of occasional barter, rather than an out-and-out alliance. They're holding back as much information as possible for future bartering, perhaps."

"Yes," Hart said, "and it isn't information the Hans are giving in return, but some form of goods, or privilege. The trick would be to locate the goods. I guess I'll have to make a personal trip around among the Big Bosses."

THE HAN CITY

This conversation set me thinking. All of the Han electrophone inter-communication had been an open record to the Americans for a good many years, and the Hans were just finding it out. For centuries they had not regarded us as any sort of a menace. Unquestionably it had never occurred to them to secrete[1] their own records. Somewhere in Nu-yok or Bah-flo, or possibly in Lo-Tan itself, the record of this traitorous transaction would be more or less openly filed. If we could only get at it! I wondered if a raid might not be possible.

Bill Hearn and I talked it over with our Han-affairs Boss and his experts. There ensued several days of research, in which the Han records of the entire decade were scanned and analyzed. In the end they picked out a mass of detail, and fitted it together into a very definite picture of the great central filing office of the Hans in Nu-yok, where the entire mass of official records was kept, constantly available for instant projectoscoping to any of the city's offices, and of the system by which the information was filed.

The attempt began to look feasible, though Hart instantly turned

[1] Conceal; hide.

the idea down when I first presented it to him. It was unthinkable, he said. Sheer suicide. But in the end I persuaded him.

"I will need," I said, "Blash, who is thoroughly familiar with the Han library system; Bert Gaunt, who for years has specialized on their military offices; Bill Barker, the ray specialist, and the best swooper pilot we have." *Swoopers* are one-man and two-man ships, developed by the Americans, with skeleton backbones of inertron (during the war painted green for invisibility against the green forests below) and "bellies" of clear ultron.

"That will be Mort Gibbons," said Hart. "We've only got three swoopers left, Tony, but I'll risk one of them if you and the others will voluntarily risk your existences. But mind, I won't urge or order one of you to go. I'll spread the word to every Plant Boss at once to give you anything and everything you need in the way of equipment."

When I told Wilma of the plan, I expected her to raise violent and tearful objections, but she didn't. She was made of far sterner stuff than the women of the 20th century. Not that she couldn't weep as copiously or be just as whimsical on occasion; but she wouldn't weep for the same reasons.

She just gave me an unfathomable look, in which there seemed to be a bit of pride, and asked eagerly for the details. I confess I was somewhat disappointed that she could so courageously risk my loss, even though I was amazed at her fortitude. But later I was to learn how little I knew her then.

We were ready to slide off at dawn the next morning. I had kissed Wilma goodbye at our camp, and after a final conference over our plans, we boarded our craft and gently glided away over the treetops on a course, which, after crossing three routes of the Han ships, would take us out over the Atlantic, off the Jersey coast, whence we would come up on Nu-yok from the ocean.

Twice we had to nose down and lie motionless on the ground near a route while Han ships passed. Those were tense moments. Had the green back of our ship been observed, we would have been disintegrated in a second. But it wasn't.

Once over the water, however, we climbed in a great spiral, ten miles in diameter, until our altimeter registered ten miles.

Here Gibbons shut off his rocket motor, and we floated, far above the level of the Atlantic liners, whose course was well to the north of us anyhow, and waited for nightfall.

Then Gibbons turned from his control long enough to grin at me.

"I have a surprise for you, Tony," he said, throwing back the lid of what I had supposed was a big supply case. And with a sigh of relief, Wilma stepped out of the case.

"If you 'go into zero' (a common expression of the day for being annihilated by the disintegrator ray), you don't think I'm going to let you go alone, do you, Tony? I couldn't believe my ears last night when you spoke of going without me, until I realized that you are still five hundred years behind the times in lots of ways. Don't you know, dear heart, that you offered me the greatest insult a husband could give a wife? You didn't, of course."

The others, it seemed, had all been in on the secret, and now they would have kidded me unmercifully, except that Wilma's eyes blazed dangerously.

At nightfall, we maneuvered to a position directly above the city. This took some time and calculation on the part of Bill Barker, who explained to me that he had to determine our point by ultronic bearings. The slightest resort to an electronic instrument, he feared, might be detected by our enemies' locators. In fact, we did not dare bring our swooper any lower than five miles for fear that its capacity might be reflected in their instruments.

Finally, however, he succeeded in locating above the central tower of the city.

"If my calculations are as much as ten feet off," he remarked with confidence, "I'll eat the tower. Now the rest is up to you, Mort. See what you can do to hold her steady. No—here, watch this indicator—the red beam, not the green one. See—if you keep it exactly centered on the needle, you're O.K. The width of the beam represents seventeen feet. The tower platform is fifty feet square, so we've got a good margin to work on."

For several moments we watched as Gibbons bent over his levers, constantly adjusting them with deft touches of his fingers. After a bit of wavering, the beam remained centered on the needle.

"Now," I said, "let's drop."

ch. ends p. 56

I opened the trap and looked down, but quickly shut it again when I felt the air rushing out of the ship into the rarefied atmosphere in a torrent. Gibbons literally yelled a protest from his instrument board.

"I forgot," I mumbled. "Silly of me. Of course, we'll have to drop out of compartment."

The compartment, to which I referred, was similar to those in some of the 20th century submarines. We all entered it. There was barely room for us to stand, shoulder to shoulder. With some struggles, we got into our special air helmets and adjusted the pressure. At our signal, Gibbons exhausted the air in the compartment, pumping it into the body of the ship, and as the little signal light flashed, Wilma threw open the hatch.

Setting the ultron-wire reel, I climbed through, and began to slide down gently.

We all had our belts on, of course, adjusted to a weight balance of but a few ounces. And the five-mile reel of ultron wire that was to be our guide, was of gossamer fineness, though, anyway, I believe it would have lifted the full weight of the five of us, so strong and tough was this invisible metal. As an extra precaution, since the wire was of the purest metal, and therefore totally invisible, even in daylight, we all had our belts hooked on small rings that slid down the wire.

I went down with the end of the wire. Wilma followed a few feet above me, then Barker, Gaunt, and Blash. Gibbons, of course, stayed behind to hold the ship in position and control the paying out of the line. We all had our ultrophones in place inside our air helmets, and so could converse with one another and with Gibbons. But at Wilma's suggestion, although we would have liked to let the Big Boss listen in, we kept them adjusted to short-range work, for fear that those who had been clearing with the Hans, and against whom we were on a raid for evidence, might also pick up our conversation. We had no fear that the Hans would hear us. In fact, we had the added advantage that, even after we landed, we could converse freely without danger of their hearing our voices through our air helmets.

For a while I could see nothing below but utter darkness.

Then I realized, from the feel of the air as much as from anything, that we were sinking through a cloud layer. We passed through two more cloud layers before anything was visible to us.

Then there came under my gaze, about two miles below, one of the most beautiful sights I have ever seen; the soft, yet brilliant, radiance of the great Han city of Nu-yok. Every foot of its structural members seemed to glow with a wonderful incandescence, tower piled up on tower, and all built on the vast base-mass of the city, which, so I had been told, sheered upward from the surface of the rivers to a height of 728 levels.

The city, I noticed with some surprise, did not cover anything like the same area as the New York of the 20th century. It occupied, as a matter of fact, only the lower half of Manhattan Island, with one section straddling the East River, and spreading out sufficiently over what once had been Brooklyn, to provide berths for the great liners and other air craft.

Straight beneath my feet was a tiny dark patch. It seemed the only spot in the entire city that was not aflame with radiance. This was the central tower, in the top floors of which were housed the vast library of record files and the main projectoscope plant.

"You can shoot the wire now," I ultrophoned Gibbons, and let go the little weighted knob. It dropped like a plummet, and we followed with considerable speed, but braking our descent with gloved hands sufficiently to see whether the knob, on which a faint light glowed as a signal for ourselves, might be observed by any Han guard or night prowler. Apparently it was not, and we again shot down with accelerated speed.

We landed on the roof of the tower without any mishap, and fortunately for our plan, in darkness. Since there was nothing above it on which it would have been worthwhile to shed illumination, or from which there was any need to observe it, the Hans had neglected to light the tower roof, or indeed to occupy it at all. This was the reason we had selected it as our landing place.

As soon as Gibbons had our word, he extinguished the knob light, and the knob, as well as the wire, became totally invisible. At our ultrophoned word, he would light it again.

ch. ends next p.

56 **ARMAGEDDON 2419 A.D.**

"No gun play now," I warned. "Swords only, and then only if absolutely necessary."

Closely bunched, and treading as lightly as only inertron-belted people could, we made our way cautiously through a door and down an inclined plane to the floor below, where Gaunt and Blash assured us the military offices were located.

Twice Barker cautioned us to stop as we were about to pass in front of mirror-like "windows" in the passage wall, and flattening ourselves to the floor, we crawled past them.

"Projectoscopes," he said. "Probably on automatic record only, at this time of night. Still, we don't want to leave any records for them to study after we're gone."

"Were you ever here before?" I asked.

"No," he replied, "but I haven't been studying their electrophone communications for seven years without being able to recognize these machines when I run across them."

9

THE FIGHT IN THE TOWER

So far we had not laid eyes on a Han. The tower seemed deserted. Blash and Gaunt, however, assured me that there would be at least one man on "duty" in the military offices, though he would probably be asleep, and two or three in the library proper and the projectoscope plant.

"We've got to put them out of commission," I said. "Did you bring the 'dope' cans, Wilma?"

"Yes," she said, "two for each. Here," and she distributed them.

We were now two levels below the roof, and at the point where we were to separate.

I did not want to let Wilma out of my sight, but it was necessary.

According to our plan, Barker was to make his way to the projectoscope plant, Blash and I to the library, and Wilma and Gaunt to the military office.

Blash and I traversed a long corridor, and paused at the great arched doorway of the library. Cautiously we peered in. Seated at three great switchboards were library operatives. Occasionally one of them would reach lazily for a lever, or sleepily push a button, as little numbered lights winked on and off. They were answering calls for electrograph and viewplate records on all sorts of subjects from all sections of the city.

I apprised my companions of the situation.

"Better wait a bit," Blash added. "The calls will lessen shortly."

Wilma reported an officer in the military office sound asleep.

"Give him the can, then," I said.

Barker was to do nothing more than keep watch in the projectoscope plant, and a few moments later he reported himself well concealed, with a splendid view of the floor.

"I think we can take a chance now," Blash said to me, and at my nod, he opened the lid of his dope can. Of course, the fumes did not affect us, through our helmets. They were absolutely without odor or visibility, and in a few seconds the librarians were unconscious. We stepped into the room.

There ensued considerable cautious observation and experiment on the part of Gaunt, working from the military office, and Blash in the library; while Wilma and I, with drawn swords and sharply attuned microphones, stood guard, and occasionally patrolled nearby corridors.

"I hear something approaching," Wilma said after a bit, with excitement in her voice. "It's a soft, gliding sound."

"That's an elevator somewhere," Barker cut in from the projectoscope floor. "Can you locate it? I can't hear it."

"It's to the east of me," she replied.

"And to my west," said I, faintly catching it. "It's between us, Wilma, and nearer you than me. Be careful. Have you got any information yet, Blash and Gaunt?"

"Getting it now," one of them replied. "Give us two minutes more."

"Keep at it then," I said. "We'll guard."

The soft, gliding sound ceased.

"I think it's very close to me," Wilma almost whispered. "Come closer, Tony. I have a feeling something is going to happen. I've never known my nerves to get taut like this without reason."

In some alarm, I launched myself down the corridor in a great leap toward the intersection whence I knew I could see her.

In the middle of my leap my ultrophone registered her gasp

of alarm. The next instant I glided to a stop at the intersection to see Wilma backing toward the door of the military office, her sword red with blood, and an inert form on the corridor floor. Two other Hans were circling to either side of her with wicked-looking knives, while a third evidently a high officer, judging by the resplendence of his garb tugged desperately to get an electrophone instrument out of a bulky pocket. If he ever gave the alarm, there was no telling what might happen to us.

I was at least seventy feet away, but I crouched low and sprang with every bit of strength in my legs. It would be more correct to say that I dived, for I reached the fellow head on, with no attempt to draw my legs beneath me.

Some instinct must have warned him, for he turned suddenly as I hurtled close to him. But by this time I had sunk close to the floor, and had stiffened myself rigidly, lest a dragging knee or foot might just prevent my reaching him. I brought my blade upward and over. It was a vicious slash that laid him open, bisecting him from groin to chin, and his dead body toppled down on me, as I slid to a tangled stop.

The other two startled, turned. Wilma leaped at one and struck him down with a side slash. I looked up at this instant, and the dazed fear on his face at the length of her leap registered vividly. The Hans knew nothing of our inertron belts, it seemed, and these leaps and dives of ours filled them with terror.

As I rose to my feet, a gory mess, Wilma, with a poise and speed which I found time to admire even in this crisis, again leaped. This time she dove head first as I had done and, with a beautifully executed thrust, ran the last Han through the throat.

Uncertainly, she scrambled to her feet, staggered queerly, and then sank gently prone on the corridor. She had fainted.

At this juncture, Blash and Gaunt reported with elation that they had the record we wanted.

"Back to the roof, everybody!" I ordered, as I picked Wilma up in my arms. With her inertron belt, she felt as light as a feather.

Gaunt joined me at once from the military office, and at the intersection of the corridor, we came upon Blash waiting for us. Barker, however, was not in evidence.

ch. ends next p.

"Where are you, Barker?" I called.

"Go ahead," he replied. "I'll be with you on the roof at once."

We came out in the open without any further mishap, and I instructed Gibbons in the ship to light the knob on the end of the ultron wire. It flashed dully a few feet away from us. Just how he had maneuvered the ship to keep our end of the line in position, without its swinging in a tremendous arc, I have never been able to understand. Had not the night been an unusually still one, he could not have checked the initial pendulum-like movements. As it was, there was considerable air current at certain of the levels, and in different directions too. But Gibbons was an expert of rare ability and sensitivity in the handling of a rocket ship, and he managed, with the aid of his delicate instruments, to sense the drifts almost before they affected the fine ultron wire, and to neutralize them with little shifts in the position of the ship.

Blash and Gaunt fastened their rings to the wire, and I hooked my own and Wilma's on, too. But on looking around, I found Barker was still missing.

"Barker, come!" I called. "We're waiting."

"Coming!" he replied, and indeed, at that instant, his figure appeared up the ramp. He chuckled as he fastened his ring to the wire, and said something about a little surprise he had left for the Hans.

"Don't reel in the wire more than a few hundred feet," I instructed Gibbons. "It will take too long to wind it in. We'll float up, and when we're aboard, we can drop it."

In order to float up, we had to dispense with a pound or two of weight apiece. We hurled our swords from us, and kicked off our shoes as Gibbons reeled up the line a bit, and then letting go of the wire, began to hum upward on our rings with increasing velocity.

The rush of air brought Wilma to, and I hastily explained to her that we had been successful. Receding far below us now, I could see our dully shining knob swinging to and fro in an ever widening arc, as it crossed and recrossed the black square of the tower roof. As an extra precaution, I ordered Gibbons to shut off the light, and to show one from the belly of the ship, for so great was our speed now, that I began to fear we would have difficulty in checking ourselves. We were literally falling upward, and with terrific acceleration.

Fortunately, we had several minutes in which to solve this difficulty, which none of us, strangely enough, had foreseen. It was Gibbons who found the answer.

"You'll be all right if all of you grab the wire tight when I give the word," he said. "First I'll start reeling it in at full speed. You won't get much of a jar, and then I'll decrease its speed again gradually, and its weight will hold you back. Are you ready? One—two—three!"

We all grabbed tightly with our gloved hands as he gave the word. We must have been rising a good bit faster than he figured, however, for it wrenched our arms considerably, and the maneuver set up a sickening pendulum motion.

For a while all we could do was swing there in an arc that may have been a quarter of a mile across, about three and a half miles above the city, and still more than a mile from our ship.

Gibbons skilfully took up the slack as our momentum pulled up the line. Then at last we had ourselves under control again, and continued our upward journey, checking our speed somewhat with our gloves.

There was not one of us who did not breathe a big sigh of relief when we scrambled through the hatch safely into the ship again, cast off the ultron line and slammed the trap shut.

Little realizing that we had a still more terrible experience to go through, we discussed the information Blash and Gaunt had between them extracted from the Han records, and the advisability of ultrophoning Hart at once.

10
THE WALLS OF HELL

The traitors were, it seemed, a degenerate gang of Americans, located a few miles north of Nu-yok on the wooded banks of the Hudson, the Sinsings. They had exchanged scraps of information to the Hans in return for several old repellor-ray machines, and the privilege of tuning in on the Han electronic power broadcast for their operation, provided their ships agreed to subject themselves to the orders of the Han traffic office, while aloft.

The rest wanted to ultrophone their news at once, since there was always danger that we might never get back to the gang with it.

I objected, however. The Sinsings would be likely to pick up our message. Even if we used the directional projector, they might have scouts out to the west and south in the big inter-gang stretches of country. They would flee to Nu-yok and escape the punishment they merited. It seemed to be vitally important that they should not, for the sake of example to other weak groups among the American gangs, as well as to prevent a crisis in which they might clear more vital information to the enemy.

"Out to sea again," I ordered Gibbons. "They'll be less likely to look for us in that direction."

"Easy, Boss, easy," he replied. "Wait until we get up a mile or two more. They must have discovered evidences of our raid by now, and their dis-ray wall may go in operation any moment."

Even as he spoke, the ship lurched downward and to one side.

"There it is!" he shouted. "Hang on, everybody. We're going to nose straight up!" And he flipped the rocket-motor control wide open.

Looking through one of the rear ports, I could see a nebulous, luminous ring, and on all sides the atmosphere took on a faint iridescence.

We were almost over the destructive range of the disintegrator-ray wall, a hollow cylinder of annihilation shooting upward from a solid ring of generators surrounding the city. It was the main defense system of the Hans, which had never been used except in periodic tests. They may or may not have suspected that an American rocket ship was within the cylinder; probably they had turned on their generators more as a precaution to prevent any reaching a position above the city.

But even at our present great height, we were in great danger. It was a question how much we might have been harmed by the rays themselves, for their effective range was not much more than seven or eight miles. The greater danger lay in the terrific downward rush of air within the cylinder to replace that which was being burned into nothingness by the continual play of the disintegrators. The air fell into the cylinder with the force of a gale. It would be rushing toward the wall from the outside with terrific force also, but, naturally, the effect was intensified on the interior.

Our ship vibrated and trembled. We had only one chance of escape—to fight our way well above the current. To drift down with it meant ultimately, and inevitably, to be sucked into the destruction wall at some lower level.

But very gradually and jerkily our upward movement, as shown on the indicators, began to increase, and after an hour of desperate struggle we were free of the maelstrom and into the rarefied upper levels. The terror beneath us was now invisible through several layers of cloud formations.

Gibbons brought the ship back to an even keel, and drove her eastward into one of the most brilliantly gorgeous sunrises I have ever seen.

We described a great circle to the south and west, in a long easy dive, for he had cut out his rocket motors to save them as much as possible. We had drawn terrifically on their fuel reserves in our battle with the elements. For the moment, the atmosphere below cleared, and we could see the Jersey coast far beneath, like a great map.

"We're not through yet," remarked Gibbons suddenly, pointing at his periscope, and adjusting it to telescopic focus. "A Han ship, and a 'drop ship' at that—and he's seen us. If he whips that beam of his on us, we're done."

I gazed, fascinated, at the viewplate. What I saw was a cigar-shaped ship not dissimilar to our own in design, and from the proportional size of its ports, of about the same size as our swoopers. We learned later that they carried crews, for the most part of not more than three or four men. They had streamline hulls and tails that embodied universal-jointed double fishtail rudders. In operation they rose to great heights on their powerful repellor rays, then gathered speed either by a straight nose dive, or an inclined dive in which they sometimes used the repellor ray slanted at a sharp angle. He was already above us, though several miles to the north. He could, of course, try to get on our tail and "spear" us with his beam as he dropped at us from a great height.

Suddenly his beam blazed forth in a blinding flash, whipping downward slowly to our right. He went through a peculiar cork-screw-like evolution, evidently maneuvering to bring his beam to bear on us with a spiral motion.

Gibbons instantly sent our ship into a series of evolutions that must have looked like those of a frightened hen. Alternately, he used the forward and the reverse rocket blasts, and in varying degree. We fluttered, we shot suddenly to right and left, and dropped like a plummet in uncertain movements. But all the time the Han scout dropped toward us, determinedly whipping the air around us with his beam. Once it sliced across beneath us, not more than a hundred feet, and we dropped with a jar into the pocket formed by the destruction of the air.

ch. ends next p.

He had dropped to within a mile of us, and was coming with the speed of a projectile, when the end came. Gibbons always swore it was sheer luck. Maybe it was, but I like pilots who are lucky that way.

In the midst of a dizzy, fluttering maneuver of our own, with the Han ship enlarging to our gaze with terrifying rapidity, and its beam slowly slicing toward us in what looked like certain destruction within the second, I saw Gibbons' fingers flick at the lever of his rocket gun and a split second later the Han ship flew apart like a clay pigeon.

We staggered, and fluttered crazily for several moments while Gibbons struggled to bring our ship into balance, and a section of about four square feet in the side of the ship near the stern slowly crumbled like rusted metal. His beam actually had touched us, but our explosive rocket had got him a thousandth of a second sooner.

Part of our rudder had been annihilated, and our motor damaged. But we were able to swoop gently back across Jersey, fortunately crossing the ship lanes without sighting any more Han craft, and finally settling to rest in the little glade beneath the trees, near Hart's camp.

11

THE NEW BOSS

We had ultrophoned our arrival and the Big Boss himself, surrounded by the Council, was on hand to welcome us and learn our news. In turn we were informed that during the night a band of raiding Bad Bloods, disguised under the insignia of the Altoonas, a gang some distance to the west of us, had destroyed several of our camps before our people had rallied and driven them off. Their purpose, evidently, had been to embroil us with the Altoonas, but fortunately, one of our exchanges recognized the Bad Blood leader, who had been slain.

The Big Boss had mobilized the full raiding force of the Gang, and was on the point of heading an expedition for the extermination of the Bad Bloods.

I looked around the grim circle of the sub-bosses, and realized the fate of America, at this moment, lay in their hands. Their temper demanded the immediate expenditure of our full effort in revenging ourselves for this raid. But the strategic exigencies, to my mind, quite clearly demanded the instant and absolute extermination of the Sinsings. It might be only a matter of hours, for all we knew, before these degraded people would barter clues to the American ultronic secrets to the Hans.

"How large a force have we?" I asked Hart.

"Every man and maid who can be spared," he replied. "That gives us seven hundred married and unmarried men, and three hundred girls, more than the entire Bad Blood Gang. Everyone is equipped with belts, ultrophones, rocket guns, and swords, and all fighting mad."

I meditated how I might put the matter to these determined men, and was vaguely conscious that they were awaiting my words.

Finally I began to speak. I do not remember to this day just what I said. I talked calmly, with due regard for their passion, but with deep conviction. I went over the information we had collected, point by point, building my case logically, and painting a lurid picture of the danger impending in that half-alliance between the Sinsings and the Hans of Nu-yok. I became impassioned, culminating, I believe, with a vow to proceed single-handed against the hereditary enemies of our race, "if the Wyomings were blindly set on placing a gang feud ahead of honor and duty and the hopes of all America."

As I concluded, a great calm came over me, as of one detached. I had felt much the same way during several crises in the First World War. I gazed from face to face, striving to read their expressions, and in a mood to make good my threat without any further heroics, if the decision was against me.

But it was Hart who sensed the temper of the Council more quickly than I did, and looked beyond it into the future.

He arose from the tree trunk on which he had been sitting.

"That settles it," he said, looking around the ring. "I have felt this thing coming on for some time now. I'm sure the Council agrees with me that there is among us a man more capable than I, to boss the Wyoming Gang, despite his handicap of having had all too short a time in which to familiarize himself with our modern ways and facilities. Whatever I can do to support his effective leadership, at any cost, I pledge myself to do."

As he concluded, he advanced to where I stood, and taking from his head the green-crested helmet that constituted his badge of office, to my surprise he placed it in my mechanically extended hand.

The roar of approval that went up from the Council members left me dazed. Somebody ultrophoned the news to the rest of the Gang, and even though the earflaps of my helmet were turned up, I could hear the cheers with which my invisible followers greeted me, from near and distant hillsides, camps, and plants.

My first move was to make sure that the Phone Boss, in communicating this news to the members of the Gang, had not re-broadcast my talk nor mentioned my plan of shifting the attack from the Bad Bloods to the Sinsings. I was relieved by his assurance that he had not, for it would have wrecked the whole plan. Everything depended upon our ability to surprise the Sinsings.

So I pledged the Council and my companions to secrecy, and allowed it to be believed that we were about to take to the air and the trees against the Bad Bloods.

That outfit must have been badly scared, the way they were "burning" the ether with ultrophone alibis and propaganda for the benefit of the more distant gangs. It was their old game, and the only method by which they had avoided extermination long ago from their immediate neighbors—these appeals to the spirit of American brotherhood, addressed to gangs too far away to have had the sort of experience with them that had fallen to our lot.

I chuckled. Here was another good reason for the shift in my plans. Were we actually to undertake the exterminations of the Bad Bloods at once, it would have been a hard job to convince some of the gangs that we had not been precipitate and unjustified. Jealousies and prejudices existed. There were gangs which would give the benefit of the doubt to the Bad Bloods, rather than to ourselves, and the issue was now hopelessly beclouded with the clever lies that were being broadcast in an unceasing stream.

But the extermination of the Sinsings would be another thing. In the first place, there would be no warning of our action until it was all over, I hoped. In the second place, we would have indisputable proof, in the form of their rep-ray ships and other paraphernalia, of their traffic with the Hans; and the state of American prejudice, at the time of which I write held trafficking with the Hans a far more heinous thing than even a vicious gang feud.

ch. ends p. 74

I called an executive session of the Council at once. I wanted to inventory our military resources.

I created a new office on the spot, that of "Control Boss," and appointed Ned Garlin to the post, turning over his former responsibility as Plants Boss to his assistant. I needed someone, I felt, to tie in the records of the various functional activities of the campaign, and take over from me the task of keeping the records of them up to the minute.

I received reports from the bosses of the ultrophone unit, and those of food, transportation, fighting gear, chemistry, electronic activity and electrophone intelligence, ultroscopes, air patrol and contact guard.

My ideas for the campaign, of course, were somewhat tinged with my 20th century experience, and I found myself faced with the task of working out a staff organization that was a composite of the best and most easily applied principles of business and military efficiency, as I knew them from the viewpoint of immediate practicality.

What I wanted was an organization that would be specialized, functionally, not as that indicated above, but from the angles of: intelligence as to the Sinsings' activities; intelligence as to Han activities; perfection of communication with my own units; cooperation of field command; and perfect mobilization of emergency supplies and resources.

It took several hours of hard work with the Council to map out the plan. First we assigned functional experts and equipment to each "Division" in accordance with its needs. Then these in turn were reassigned by the new Division Bosses to the Field Commands as needed, or as Independent or Headquarters Units. The two intelligence divisions were named the White and the Yellow, indicating that one specialized on the American enemy and the other on the Mongolians.

The division in charge of our own communications, the assignment of ultrophone frequencies and strengths, and the maintenance of operators and equipment, I called "Communications."

I named Bill Hearn to the post of Field Boss, in charge of the main or undetached fighting units, and to the Resources Division,

I assigned all responsibility for what few aircraft we had; and all transportation and supply problems, I assigned to "Resources." The functional bosses stayed with this division.

We finally completed our organization with the assignment of liaison representatives among the various divisions as needed.

Thus I had a "Headquarters Staff" composed of the Division Bosses who reported directly to Ned Garlin as Control Boss, or to Wilma as my personal assistant. And each of the Division Bosses had a small staff of his own.

In the final summing up of our personnel and resources, I found we had roughly a thousand "troops," of whom some three hundred and fifty were, in what I called the Service Divisions, the rest being in Bill Hearn's Field Division. This latter number, however, was cut down somewhat by the assignment of numerous small units to detached service. Altogether, the actual available fighting force, I figured, would number about five hundred, by the time we actually went into action.

We had only six small swoopers, but I had an ingenious plan in my mind, as the result of our little raid on Nu-yok, that would make this sufficient, since the reserves of inertron blocks were larger than I expected to find them. The Resources Division, by packing its supply cases a bit tight, or by slipping in extra blocks of inertron, was able to reduce each to a weight of a few ounces. These easily could be floated and towed by the swoopers in any quantity. Hitched to ultron lines, it would be a virtual impossibility for them to break loose.

The entire personnel, of course, was supplied with jumpers, and if each man and girl was careful to adjust balances properly, the entire number could also be towed along through the air, grasping wires of ultron, swinging below the swoopers, or stringing out behind them.

There would be nothing tiring about this, because the strain would be no greater than that of carrying a one or two pound weight in the hand, except for air friction at high speeds. But to make doubly sure that we should lose none of our personnel, I gave strict orders that the belts and tow lines should be equipped with rings and hooks.

ch. ends p. 74

So great was the efficiency of the fundamental organization and discipline of the Gang, that we got under way at nightfall.

One by one the swoopers eased into the air, each followed by its long train or "kite-tail" of humanity and supply cases hanging lightly from its tow line. For convenience, the tow lines were made of an alloy of ultron which, unlike the metal itself, is visible.

At first these "tails" hung downward, but as the ships swung into formation and headed eastward toward the Bad Blood territory, gathering speed, they began to string out behind. And swinging low from each ship on heavily weighted lines, ultroscope, ultrophone, and straight-vision observers keenly scanned the countryside, while intelligence men in the swoopers above bent over their instrument boards and viewplates.

Leaving Control Boss Ned Garlin temporarily in charge of affairs, Wilma and I dropped a weighted line from our ship, and slid down about half way to the under lookouts, that is to say, about a thousand feet. The sensation of floating swiftly through the air like this, in the absolute security of one's confidence in the inertron belt, was one of never-ending delight to me.

We reascended into the swooper as the expedition approached the territory of the Bad Bloods, and directed the preparations for the bombardment. It was part of my plan to appear to carry out the attack as originally planned.

About fifteen miles from their camps our ships came to a halt and maintained their positions for a while with the idling blasts of their rocket motors, to give the ultroscope operators a chance to make a thorough examination of the territory below us, for it was very important that this next step in our program should be carried out with all secrecy.

At length they reported the ground below us entirely clear of any appearance of human occupation, and a gun unit of long-range specialists was lowered with a dozen rocket guns, equipped with special automatic devices that the Resources Division had developed at my request, a few hours before our departure. These were aiming and timing devices. After calculating the range, elevation and rocket charges carefully, the guns were left, concealed in a ravine, and the men were hauled up into the ship again. At the predetermined hour, those unmanned rocket guns would begin automatically to bombard the Bad Bloods' hillsides, shifting their aim and elevation slightly with each shot, as did many of our artillery pieces in the First World War.

In the meantime, we turned south about twenty miles, and grounded, waiting for the bombardment to begin before we attempted to sneak across the Han ship lane. I was relying for security on the distraction that the bombardment might furnish the Han observers.

It was tense work waiting, but the affair went through as planned, our squadron drifting across the route high enough to enable the ships' tails of troops and supply cases to clear the ground.

In crossing the second ship route, out along the Beaches of Jersey, we were not so successful in escaping observation. A Han ship came speeding along at a very low elevation. We caught it on our electronic location and direction finders, and also located it with our ultroscopes, but it came so fast and so low that I thought it best to remain where we had grounded the second time, and lie quiet, rather than get under way and cross in front of it.

The point was this: while the Hans had no such devices as our ultroscopes, with which we could see in the dark (within certain limitations of course), and their electronic instruments would be virtually useless in uncovering our presence, since all but natural electronic activities were carefully eliminated from our apparatus, except electrophone receivers (which are not easily spotted), the Hans did have some very highly sensitive sound devices which operated with great efficiency in calm weather, so far as sounds emanating from the air were concerned. But the "ground roar" greatly confused their use of these instruments in the location of specific sounds floating up from the surface of the earth.

This ship must have caught some slight noise of ours, however, in its sensitive instruments, for we heard its electronic devices go into play, and picked up the routine report of the noise to its Base Ship Commander. But from the nature of the conversation, I judged they had not identified it, and were, in fact, more curious about the detonations they were picking up now from the Bad Blood lands some sixty miles or so to the west.

ch. ends next p.

Immediately after this ship had shot by, we took the air again, and following much the same route that I had taken the previous night, climbed in a long semi-circle out over the ocean, swung toward the north and finally the west. We set our course, however, for the Sinsings' land north of Nu-yok, instead of for the city itself.

12

THE FINGER OF DOOM

As we crossed the Hudson River, a few miles north of the city, we dropped several units of the Yellow Intelligence Division, with full instrumental equipment. Their apparatus cases were nicely balanced at only a few ounces weight each, and the men used their chute capes to ease their drops.

We recrossed the river a little distance above and began dropping White Intelligence units and a few long and short range gun units. Then we held our position until we began to get reports. Gradually we ringed the territory of the Sinsings, our observation units working busily and patiently at their locators and scopes, both aloft and aground, until Garlin finally turned to me with the remark: "The map circle is complete now, Boss. We've got clear locations all the way around them."

"Let me see it," I replied, and studied the illuminated viewplate map, with its little overlapping circles of light that indicated spots proved clear of the enemy by ultroscopic observation.

I nodded to Bill Hearn. "Go ahead now, Hearn," I said, "and place your barrage men."

He spoke into his ultrophone, and three of the ships began to glide in a wide ring around the enemy territory. Every few seconds, at the word from his Unit Boss, a gunner would drop off the wire, and slipping the clasp of his chute cape, drift down into the darkness below.

Bill formed two lines, parallel to and facing the river, and enclosing the entire territory of the enemy between them. Above and below, straddling the river, were two defensive lines. These latter were merely to hold their positions. The others were to close in toward each other, pushing a high-explosive barrage five miles ahead of them. When the two barrages met, both lines were to switch to short-vision-range barrage and continue to close in on any of the enemy who might have drifted through the previous curtain of fire.

In the meantime, Bill kept his reserves, a picked corps of a hundred men (the same that had accompanied Hart and myself in our fight with the Han squadron) in the air, divided about equally among the "kite-tails" of four ships.

A final roll call, by units, companies, divisions and functions, established the fact that all our forces were in position. No Han activity was reported, and no Han broadcasts indicated any suspicion of our expedition. Nor was there any indication that the Sinsings had any knowledge of the fate in store for them. The idling of rep-ray generators was reported from the center of their camp, obviously those of the ships the Hans had given them—the price of their treason to their race.

Again I gave the word, and Hearn passed on the order to his subordinates.

Far below us, and several miles to the right and left, the two barrage lines made their appearance. From the great height to which we had risen, they appeared like lines of brilliant, winking lights, and the detonations were muffled by the distances into a sort of rumbling, distant thunder. Hearn and his assistants were very busy: measuring, calculating, and snapping out ultrophone orders to unit commanders that resulted in the straightening of lines and the closing of gaps in the barrage.

The White Division Boss reported the utmost confusion in the Sinsing organization. They were, as might be expected, an inefficient, loosely disciplined gang, and repeated broadcasts for help to neighboring gangs. Ignoring the fact that the Mongolians had not used explosives for many generations, they nevertheless jumped at the conclusion that they were being raided by the Hans. Their frantic broadcasts persisted in this thought, despite the nervous electrophonic inquiries of the Hans themselves, to whom the sound of the battle was evidently audible, and who were trying to locate the trouble.

At this point, the swooper I had sent south toward the city went into action as a diversion, to keep the Hans at home. Its "kite-tail" loaded with long-range gunners, using the most highly explosive rockets we had, hung invisible in the darkness of the sky and bombarded the city from a distance of about five miles. With an entire city to shoot at, and the object of creating as much commotion therein as possible, regardless of actual damage, the gunners had no difficulty in hitting the mark. I could see the glow of the city and the stabbing flashes of exploding rockets. In the end, the Hans, uncertain as to what was going on, fell back on a defensive policy, and shot their "hell cylinder," or wall of upturned disintegrator rays into operation. That, of course, ended our bombardment of them. The rays were a perfect defense, disintegrating our rockets as they were reached.

If they had not sent out ships before turning on the rays, and if they had none within sufficient radius already in the air, all would be well.

I queried Garlin on this, but he assured me Yellow Intelligence reported no indications of Han ships nearer than 800 miles. This would probably give us a free hand for a while, since most of their instruments recorded only imperfectly or not at all, through the death wall.

Requisitioning one of the viewplates of the headquarters ship, and the services of an expert operator, I instructed him to focus on our lines below. I wanted a close-up of the men in action.

He began to manipulate his controls and chaotic shadows moved rapidly across the plate, fading in and out of focus, until he reached an adjustment that gave me a picture of the forest floor, apparently 100 feet wide, with the intervening branches and foliage

ch. ends p. 81

of the trees appearing like shadows that melted into reality a few feet above the ground.

I watched one man setting up his long-gun with skillful speed. His lips pursed slightly as though he were whistling, as he adjusted the tall tripod on which the long tube was balanced. Swiftly he twirled the knobs controlling the aim and elevation of his piece. Then, lifting a belt of ammunition from the big box, which itself looked heavy enough to break down the spindly tripod, he inserted the end of it in the lock of his tube and touched the proper combination of buttons.

Then he stepped aside, and occupied himself with peering carefully through the trees ahead. Not even a tremor shook the tube, but I knew that at intervals of something less than a second, it was discharging small projectiles which, traveling under their own continuously reduced power, were arching into the air, to fall precisely five miles ahead and explode with the force of eight-inch shells, such as we used in the First World War.

Another gunner, fifty feet to the right of him, waved a hand and called out something to him. Then, picking up his own tube and tripod, he gaged the distance between the trees ahead of him, and the height of their lowest branches, and bending forward a bit, flexed his muscles and leaped lightly, some twenty-five feet. Another leap took him another twenty feet or so, where he began to set up his piece.

I ordered my observer then to switch to the barrage itself. He got a close focus on it, but this showed little except a continuous series of blinding flashes, which, from the viewplate, lit up the entire interior of the ship. An eight-hundred-foot focus proved better. I had thought that some of our French and American artillery of the 20th century had achieved the ultimate in mathematical precision of fire, but I had never seen anything to equal the accuracy of that line of terrific explosions as it moved steadily forward, mowing down trees as a scythe cuts grass (or used to 500 years ago), literally churning up the earth and the splintered, blasted remains of the forest giants, to a depth of from ten to twenty feet.

By now the two curtains of fire were nearing each other, lines of vibrant, shimmering, continuous, brilliant destruction, inevitably squeezing the panic-stricken Sinsings between them.

Even as I watched, a group of them, who had been making a futile effort to get their three rep-ray machines into the air, abandoned their efforts, and rushed forth into the milling mob.

I queried the Control Boss sharply on the futility of this attempt of theirs, and learned that the Hans, apparently in doubt as to what was going on, had continued to "play safe," and broken off their power broadcast, after ordering all their own ships east of the Alleghenies to the ground, for fear these ships they had traded to the Sinsings might be used against them.

Again I turned to my viewplate, which was still focussed on the central section of the Sinsing works. The confusion of the traitors was entirely that of fear, for our barrage had not yet reached them.

Some of them set up their long-guns and fired at random over the barrage line, then gave it up. They realized that they had no target to shoot at, no way of knowing whether our gunners were a few hundred feet or several miles beyond it.

Their ultrophone men, of whom they did not have many, stood around in tense attitudes, their helmet phones strapped around their ears, nervously fingering the tuning controls at their belts. Unquestionably they must have located some of our frequencies, and overheard many of our reports and orders. But they were confused and disorganized. If they had an Ultrophone Boss they evidently were not reporting to him in an organized way.

They were beginning to draw back now before our advancing fire. With intermittent desperation, they began to shoot over our barrage again, and the explosions of their rockets flashed at widely scattered points beyond. A few took distance "pot shots."

Oddly enough it was our own forces that suffered the first casualties in the battle. Some of these distance shots by chance registered hits, while our men were under strict orders not to exceed their barrage distances.

Seen upon the ultroscope viewplate, the battle looked as though it were being fought in daylight, perhaps on a cloudy day, while the explosions of the rockets appeared as flashes of extra brilliance.

The two barrage lines were not more than five hundred feet

ch. ends next p.

apart when the Sinsings resorted to tactics we had not foreseen. We noticed first that they began to lighten themselves by throwing away extra equipment. A few of them in their excitement threw away too much, and shot suddenly into the air. Then a scattering few floated up gently, followed by increasing numbers, while still others, preserving a weight balance, jumped toward the closing barrages and leaped high, hoping to clear them. Some succeeded. We saw others blown about like leaves in a windstorm, to crumple and drift slowly down, or else to fall into the barrage, their belts blown from their bodies.

However, it was not part of our plan to allow a single one of them to escape and find his way to the Hans. I quickly passed the word to Bill Hearn to have the alternate men in his line raise their barrages and heard him bark out a mathematical formula to the Unit Bosses.

We backed off our ships as the explosions climbed into the air in stagger formation until they reached a height of three miles. I don't believe any of the Sinsings who tried to float away to freedom succeeded.

But we did know later, that a few who leaped the barrage got away and ultimately reached Nu-yok.

It was those who managed to jump the barrage who gave us the most trouble. With half of our long-guns turned aloft, I foresaw we would not have enough to establish successive ground barrages and so ordered the barrage back two miles, from which positions our "curtains" began to close in again, this time, however, gaged to explode, not on contact, but thirty feet in the air. This left little chance for the Sinsings to leap either over or under it.

Gradually, the two barrages approached each other until they finally met, and in the gray dawn the battle ended.

Our own casualties amounted to forty-seven men in the ground forces, eighteen of whom had been slain in hand-to-hand fighting with the few of the enemy who managed to reach our lines, and sixty-two in the crew and "kite-tail" force of swooper No. 4, which had been located by one of the enemy's ultroscopes and brought down with long-gun fire.

Since nearly every member of the Sinsing Gang had, so far as we knew, been killed, we considered the raid a great success.

It had, however, a far greater significance than this. To all of us who took part in the expedition, the effectiveness of our barrage tactics definitely established a confidence in our ability to overcome the Hans.

As I pointed out to Wilma: "It has been my belief all along, dear, that the American explosive rocket is a far more efficient weapon than the disintegrator ray of the Hans, once we can train all our gangs to use it systematically and in coordinated fashion. As a weapon in the hands of a single individual, shooting at a mark in direct line of vision, the rocket-gun is inferior in destructive power to the dis-ray, except as its range may be a little greater. The trouble is that to date it has been used only as we used our rifles and shotguns in the 20th century. The possibilities of its use as artillery, in laying barrages that advance along the ground, or climb into the air, are tremendous.

"The dis-ray inevitably reveals its source of emanation. The rocket gun does not. The dis-ray can reach its target only in a straight line. The rocket may be made to travel in an arc, over intervening obstacles, to an unseen target.

"Nor must we forget that our ultronists now are promising us a perfect shield against the dis-ray in inertron."

"I tremble though, Tony dear, when I think of the horrors that are ahead of us. The Hans are clever. They will develop defenses against our new tactics. And they are sure to mass against us not only the full force of their power in America, but the united forces of the World Empire. They are a cowardly race in one sense, but clever as the very Devils in Hell, and inheritors of a calm, ruthless, vicious persistency."

"Nevertheless," I prophesied, "the Finger of Doom points squarely at them today, and unless you and I are killed in the struggle, we shall live to see America blast the Yellow Blight from the face of the Earth."

AFTERWORD

The August 1928 issue of *Amazing Stories* was beyond question one of the most important not only in its history but in the history of science fiction. That would have been the case if it had only presented to the science fiction public a new author named Edward Elmer Smith with the first installment of *The Skylark of Space*. But its immortality was assured by introducing Anthony "Buck "Rogers to the world in a 25,000 word novelette titled *Armageddon 2419 A.D.*, by Philip Francis Nowlan.

Few people, either in or out of science fiction, know that "Buck" Rogers was born in *Amazing Stories*. Fewer still are aware that the first artist to cartoon the famous future Americans and soldiers of Han was Frank R. Paul.[1] Breaking its policy, *Amazing Stories* ran, in addition to two full-size illustrations, three cartoon panels which may even have given Nowlan the idea of submitting the entire package to a comic strip syndicate.

When *Buck Rogers in the Twenty-Fifth Century* appeared as a comic strip in the daily newspapers in 1929 it created a sensation

---

[1] Frank Rudolph Paul (1884–1963) was an American illustrator of science fiction pulp magazines. Discovered by Gernsback, Paul was influential in defining the look of both cover art and interior illustrations in the nascent science fiction pulps of the 1920s. He was inducted into the Science Fiction Hall of Fame in 2009.

and added a new phrase to the language. Phil Nowlan wrote the continuity about the famous characters of Buck Rogers, Wilma Deering, Dr. Huer, and Killer Kane, along with their disintegrators, jumping belts, inertron, and paralysis rays, and made them familiar to millions of people in this country and abroad. The daily adventures on radio thrilled many more. The popularity of the strip began to decline in the late thirties under the competition of Flash Gordon, Brick Bradford, and other imitators. When Phil Nowlan severed his connection with the strip there was a steady loss of readership. Today, though the strip still appears in some papers, few people are aware it still exists. When Nowlan left the strip in 1939 he resumed his writing of magazine science fiction; but he died in early 1940.

"Buck Rogers" is a synonym for the world of tomorrow, future invention and the spirit of science fiction. In past years the phrase "that Buck Rogers stuff" had a derisive ring to it, but more recently atom bombs and earth satellites have changed all that.

The strangest part about this entire story is that the original Buck Rogers' stories in *Amazing Stories* were in no sense juvenile. They were serious, adult works based on the most plausible science of the time. They have an aura of accurate prophecy about them that cannot be erased. *Armageddon 2419 A.D.* precisely described the bazooka, the jet plane, walkie-talkie for warfare, the infrared ray gun for fighting at night, as well as dozens of other advances that are not here yet but are on their way. The perceptive Hugo Gernsback, then editor and publisher of *Amazing* called his shots as accurately on the quality of his stories as he did on future invention. Of *Armageddon 2419 A.D.* he said: "We have rarely printed a story in this magazine that for scientific interest as well as suspense could hold its own with this particular story. We prophesy that this story will become more valuable as the years go by. It certainly holds a number of interesting prophecies, many of which, no doubt, will come true. For wealth of science it will be hard to beat for some time to come. It is one of those rare stories that will bear reading and rereading many times."

Cele Goldsmith
Amazing Stories
April 1961

If you have read *Armageddon 2419 A.D.*—and we are sure you have—you may have a slight idea what is in store for you in the present sequel.

Mr. Nowlan has quite outdone himself. In our humble opinion, the sequel is in many respects better than the original story.

We hope that will be your verdict also.

Like the first story, this one is pregnant with adventure, mystery, and science to an unusual degree for stories of this kind.

Apparently Mr. Nowlan has developed an entirely new technique in inventing new and amazing instrumentatlities, and indeed, wholly new branches of science itself, particularly science as applied to warfare. And no matter how fast a thinker and no matter how good a scientist you are, you will find that the author is always a few steps ahead of you and anticipates your own thoughts nine times out of ten.

It is a capital story which you will enjoy all the way through.

Hugo Gernsback
Amazing Stories
March 1929

PHILIP FRANCIS NOWLAN

THE AIRLORDS OF HAN

THE FIRST
BUCK ROGERS
SEQUEL

1

THE AIRLORDS BESIEGED

In a previous record of my adventures in the early part of the Second War of Independence I explained how I, Anthony Rogers, was overcome by radioactive gases in an abandoned mine near Scranton in the year 1927, where I existed in a state of suspended animation for nearly five hundred years; and awakened to find that the America I knew had been crushed under the cruel tyranny of the Airlords of Han, fierce Mongolians, who, as scientists now contend, had in their blood a taint not of this earth, and who with science and resources far in advance of those of a United States, economically prostrate at the end of a long series of wars with a Bolshevik Europe, in the year 2270 A.D., had swept down from the skies in their great airships that rode "repellor rays" as a ball rides the stream of a fountain, and with their terrible "disintegrator rays" had destroyed more than four-fifths of the American race, and driven the other fifth to cover in the vast forests which grew up over the remains of the once mighty civilization of the United States.

I explained the part I played in the fall of the year 2419, when the rugged Americans, with science secretly developed to terrific efficiency in their forest fastness, turned fiercely and assumed the aggressive against a now effete[1] Han population, which for generations had shut itself up in the fifteen great Mongolian cities of America, having abandoned cultivation of the soil and the operation of mines; for these Hans produced all they needed in the way of food, clothing, shelter and machinery through electrono-synthetic processes.

I explained how I was adopted into the Wyoming Gang, or clan, descendants of the original populations of Wilkes-Barre, Scranton, and the Wyoming Valley in Pennsylvania; how quite by accident I stumbled upon a method of destroying Han aircraft by shooting explosive rockets, not directly at the heavily armored ships, but at the repellor ray columns, which automatically drew the rockets upward where they exploded in the generators of the aircraft; how the Wyomings threw the first thrill of terror into the Airlords by bringing an entire squadron crashing to earth; how a handful of us in a rocketship successfully raided the Han city of Nu-Yok; and how by the application of military principles I remembered from the First World War, I was able to lead the Wyomings to victory over the Sinsings, a Hudson River tribe which had formed a traitorous alliance with the hereditary enemies and oppressors of the White Race in America.

By the Spring of 2420 A.D., a short six months after these events, the positions of the Yellow and the White Races in America had been reversed. The hunted were now the hunters. The Hans desperately were increasing the defenses of their fifteen cities, around each of which the American Gangs had drawn a widely deployed line of long-gunners; while nervous air convoys, closely bunched behind their protective screen of disintegrator beams, kept up sporadic and costly systems of transportation between the cities.

During this period our own campaign against the Hans of Nu-Yok was fairly typical of the development of the war throughout

[1] No longer capable of effective action.

the country. Our force was composed of contingents from most of the Gangs of Pennsylvania, Jersey, and New England. We encircled the city on a wide radius, our line running roughly from Staten Island to the forested site of the ancient city of Elizabeth, to First and Second Mountains just west of the ruins of Newark, Bloomfield, and Montclair, thence northeasterly across the Hudson, and down to the Sound. On Long Island our line was pushed forward to the first slopes of the hills.

We had no more than four long-gunners to the square mile in our first line, but each of these was equal to a battery of heavy artillery such as I had known in the First World War. And when their fire was first concentrated on the Han city, they blew its outer walls and roof levels into a chaotic mass of wreckage before the nervous Yellow engineers could turn on the ring of generators which surrounded the city with a vertical film of disintegrator rays. Our explosive rockets could not penetrate this film, for it disintegrated them instantly and harmlessly, as it did all other material substance with the sole exception of "inertron," that synthetic element developed by the Americans from the sub-electronic and ultronic orders.

The continuous operation of the disintegrators destroyed the air and maintained a constant vacuum wherever they played, into which the surrounding air continuously rushed, naturally creating atmospheric disturbances after a time, which resulted in a local storm. This, however, ceased after a number of hours, when the flow of air toward the city became steady.

The Hans suffered severely from atmospheric conditions inside their city at first, but later rearranged their disintegrator ring in a system of overlapping films that left diagonal openings, through which the air rushed to them, and through which their ships emerged to scout our positions.

We shot down seven of their cruisers before they realized the folly of floating individually over our invisible line. Their beams traced paths of destruction like scars across the countryside,

ch. ends p. 94

but caught less than half a dozen of our gunners all told, for it takes a lot of time to sweep every square foot of a square mile with a beam whose cross section is not more than twenty or twenty-five feet in diameter. Our gunners, completely concealed beneath the foliage of the forest, with weapons which did not reveal their position, as did the flashes and detonation of the 20th century artillery, hit their repellor rays with comparative ease.

The "drop ships," which the Hans next sent out, were harder to handle. Rising to immense heights behind the city's disintegrator wall, these tiny, projectile-like craft slipped through the rifts in the cylinder of destruction, and then turning off their repellor rays, dropped at terrific speed until their small vanes were sufficient to support them as they volplaned[2] in great circles, shooting back into the city defenses at a lower level.

The great speed of these craft made it almost impossible to register a direct hit against them with rocket guns, and they had no repellor rays at which we might shoot while they were over our lines.

But by the same token they were able to do little damage to us. So great was the speed of a drop ship, that the only way in which it could use a disintegrator ray was from a fixed generator in the nose of the structure, as it dropped in a straight line toward its target. But since they could not sight the widely deployed individual gunners in our line, their scouting was just as ineffective as our attempts were to shoot them down.

For more than a month the situation remained a deadlock, with the Hans locked up in their cities, while we mobilized gunners and supplies.

Had our stock of inertron been sufficiently great at this period, we could have ended the war quickly, with aircraft impervious to the dis-ray. But the production of inertron is a painfully slow process, involving the building up of this weightless element from

---

[2] Make a controlled dive or downward flight, especially with the engine shut off.

ultronic vibrations through the sub-electronic, electronic, and atomic states into molecular form. Our laboratories had barely begun production on a quantity basis, for we had just learned how to protect them from Han air raids, and it would be many months more before the supply they had just started to manufacture would be finished. In the meantime we had enough for a few aircraft, for jumping belts and a small amount of armor.

We Wyomings possessed one swooper completely sheathed with inertron and counterweighted with ultron. The Altoonas and the Lycomings also had one apiece. But a shielded swooper, while impervious to the dis-ray, was helpless against squadrons of Han aircraft, for the Hans developed a technique of playing their beams underneath the swooper in such fashion as to suck it down flutteringly into the vacuum so created, until they brought it finally, and more or less violently, to earth.

Ultimately the Hans broke our blockade to a certain extent, when they resumed traffic between their cities in great convoys, protected by squadrons of cruisers in vertical formation, playing a continuous crossfire of disintegrator beams ahead of them and down on the sides in a most effective screen, so that it was very difficult for us to get a rocket through to the repellor rays.

But we lined the scar paths beneath their air routes for miles at a stretch with concealed gunners, some of whom would sooner or later register hits, and it was seldom that a convoy made the trip between Nu-Yok and Bos-Tan, Bah-Flo, Si-ka-ga or Ah-la-nah without losing several of its ships.

Hans who reached the ground alive were never taken prisoner. Not even the splendid discipline of the Americans could curb the wild hate developed through centuries of dastardly oppression, and the Hans were mercilessly slaughtered, when they did not save us the trouble by committing suicide.

Several times the Hans drove "air wedges" over our lines in this vertical or "cloud bank" formation, plowing a scar path a mile or more wide through our positions. But at worst, to us, this did not mean the loss of more than a dozen men and girls, and generally their raids cost them one or more ships. They cut paths of destruction across the map, but they could not cover the entire area,

ch. ends next p.

and when they had plowed out over our lines, there was nothing left for them to do but to turn around and plow back to Nu-Yok. Our lines closed up again after each raid, and we continued to take heavy toll from convoys and raiding fleets. Finally they abandoned these tactics.

So at the time of which I speak, the Spring of 2420 A.D., the Americans and the Hans were temporarily at a deadlock. But the Hans were as desperate as we were sanguine,[3] for we had time on our side.

It was at this period that we first learned of the Airlords' determination, a very unpopular one with their conscripted populations, to carry the fight to us on the ground. The time had passed when command of the air meant victory. We had no visible cities nor massed bodies of men for them to destroy, nothing but vast stretches of silent forests and hills, where our forces lurked, invisible from the air.

---

[3] Optimistic.

THE GROUNDSHIPS THREATEN

One of our Wyoming girls, on contact guard near Pocono, blundered into a hunting camp of the Bad Bloods, one of the renegade American Gangs, which occupied the Blue Mountain section north of Delaware Water Gap. We had not invited their cooperation in this campaign, for they were under some suspicion of having trafficked with the Hans in past years, but they had offered no objection to our passage through their territory in our advance on Nu-Yok.

Fortunately our contact guard had been able to leap into the upper branches of a tree without being discovered by the Bad Bloods, for their discipline was lax and their guard careless. She overheard enough of the conversation of their Bosses around the camp fire beneath her to indicate the general nature of the Han plans.

After several hours she was able to leap away unobserved through the topmost branches of the trees, and after putting several miles between herself and their camp, she ultrophoned a full report to her Contact Boss back in the Wyoming Valley. My own Ultrophone Field Boss picked up the message and brought the graph record of it to me at once.

Her report was likewise picked up by the Bosses of the various

Gang units in our line, and we had called a council to discuss our plans by word of mouth.

We were gathered in a sheltered glade on the eastern slope of First Mountain on a balmy night in May. Far to the east, across the forested slopes of the lowlands, the flat stretches of open meadow and the rocky ridge that once had been Jersey City, the iridescent glow of Nu-Yok's protecting film of annihilation shot upward, gradually fading into a starry sky.

In the faint glow of our ultronolamps, I made out the great figure and rugged features of Boss Casaman, commander of the Mifflin unit, and the gray uniform of Boss Warn, who led the Sandsnipers of the Barnegat Beaches, and who had swooped over from his headquarters on Sandy Hook. By his side stood Boss Handan of the Winslows, a Gang from Central Jersee. In the group also were the leaders of the Altoonas, the Camerons, the Lycomings, Susquannas, Harshbargs, Hagersduns, Chesters, Reddings, Delawares, Elmirans, Kiugas, Hudsons, and Connedigas.

Most of them were clad in forest-green uniforms that showed black at night, but each had some distinctive badge or item of uniform or equipment that distinguished his Gang.

Both the Mifflin and Altoona Bosses, for instance, wore heavy-looking boots with jointed knees. They came from sections that were not only mountainous, but rocky, where "leaping" involves many a slip and bruised limb, unless some protection of this sort is worn. But these boots were not as heavy as they looked, being counter-balanced somewhat with inertron.

The headgear of the Winslows was quite different from the close-fitting helmet of the Wyomings, being large and bushy-looking, for in the Winslow territory there were many stretches of nearly bare land, with occasional scrubby pines, and a Winslow caught in the open, on the approach of a Han airship, would twist himself into a motionless imitation of a scrubby plant, that passed very successfully for the real thing, when viewed from several thousand feet in the air.

The Susquannas had a unit that was equipped with inertron shields, that were of the same shape as those of the ancient Romans, but much larger, and capable of concealing their bearers from head to foot when they crouched slightly. These shields, of course, were colored forest green, and were irregularly shaded; they were balanced with inertron, so that their effective weight was only a few ounces. They were curious too, in that they had handles for both hands, and two small reservoir rocket-guns built into them as integral parts.

In going into action, the Susquannas crouched slightly, holding the shields before them with both hands, looking through a narrow vision slit, and working both rocket guns. The shields, however, were a great handicap in leaping, and in advancing through heavy forest growth.

The field unit of the Delawares was also heavily armored. It was one of the most efficient bodies of shock troops in our entire line. They carried circular shields, about three feet in diameter, with a vision slit and a small rocket gun. These shields were held at arm's length in the left hand on going into action. In the right hand was carried an ax-gun, an affair not unlike the battle-ax of the Middle Ages. It was about three feet long. The shaft consisted of a rocket gun, with an ax-blade near the muzzle, and a spike at the other end. It was a terrible weapon. Jointed leg-guards protected the ax-gunner below the rim of his shield, and a hemispherical helmet, the front section of which was of transparent ultron reaching down to the chin, completed his equipment.

The Susquannas also had a long-gun unit in the field.

One company of my Wyomings I had equipped with a weapon which I designed myself. It was a long-gun which I had adapted for bayonet tactics such as American troops used in the First World War, in the 20th century. It was about the length of the ancient rifle, and was fitted with a short knife bayonet. The stock, however, was replaced by a narrow ax-blade and a spike. It had two hand-guards also. It was fired from the waist position.

In hand-to-hand work, one lunged with the bayonet in a vicious, swinging up-thrust, following through with an up-thrust of the ax-blade as one rushed in on one's opponent, and then a down-thrust of the butt-spike, developing into a down-slice of the bayonet, and a final upward jerk of the bayonet at the throat and chin with

ch. ends p. 100

a shortened grip on the barrel, which had been allowed to slide through the hands at the completion of the down-slice.

I almost regretted that we would not find ourselves opposed to the Delaware ax-men in this campaign, so curious was I to compare the efficiency of the two bodies.

But both the Delawares and my own men were elated at the news that the Hans intended to fight it out on the ground at last, and the prospect that we might in consequence come to close quarters with them.

Many of the Gang Bosses were dubious about our Wyoming policy of providing our fighters with no inertron armor as protection against the disintegrator ray of the Hans. Some of them even questioned the value of all weapons intended for hand-to-hand fighting.

As Warn, of the Sandsnipers put it: "You should be in a better position than anyone, Rogers, with your memories of the 20th century, to appreciate that between the superdeadliness of the rocket gun and of the disintegrator ray there will never be any opportunity for hand-to-hand work. Long before the opposing forces could come to grips, one or the other will be wiped out."

But I only smiled, for I remembered how much of this same talk there was five centuries ago, and that it was even predicted in 1914 that no war could last more than six months.

That there would be hand-to-hand work before we were through, and in plenty, I was convinced, and so every able-bodied youth I could muster was enrolled in my infantry battalion and spent most of his time in vigorous bayonet practice. And for the same reason I had discarded the idea of armor. I felt it would be clumsy, and questioned its value. True, it was an absolute bar against the disintegrator ray, but of what use would that be if a Han ray found a crevice between overlapping plates, or if the ray was used to annihilate the very earth beneath the wearer's feet?

The only protective equipment that I thought was worth a whoop was a very peculiar device with which a contingent of five hundred Altoonas was supplied. They called it the "umbrashield." It was a bell-shaped affair of inertron, counterweighted with ultron, about eight feet high. The gunner, who walked inside it, carried it easily with two shoulder straps. There were handles inside too, by which the gunner might more easily balance it when running, or lift it to clear any obstructions on the ground.

In the apex of the affair, above his head, was a small turret, containing an automatic rocket gun. The periscopic gun sight and the controls were on a level with the operator's eyes. In going into action he could, after taking up his position, simply stoop until the rim of the umbra-shield rested on the ground, or else slip off the shoulder straps, and stand there, quite safe from the disintegrator ray, and work his gun.

But again, I could not see what was to prevent the Hans from slicing underneath it, instead of directly at it, with their rays.

As I saw it, any American who was unfortunate enough to get in the direct path of a dis-ray, was almost certain to "go out," unless he was locked up tight in a complete shell of inertron, as for instance, in an inertron swooper. It seemed to me better to concentrate all our efforts on tactics of attack, trusting to our ability to get the Hans before they got us.

I had one other main unit besides my bayonet battalion, a long-gun contingent composed entirely of girls, as were my scout units and most of my auxiliary contingents. These youngsters had been devoting themselves to target practice for months, and had developed a fine technique of range-finding and the various other tactics of 20th century massed artillery, to which was added the scientific perfection of the rocket guns and an average mental alertness that would have put the artilleryman of the First World War to shame.

From the information our contact guard had obtained, it appeared that the Hans had developed a type of groundship completely protected by a disintegrator ray "canopy" that was operated from a short mast, and spread down around it as a cone.

These ships were merely adaptations of their airships, and were designed to travel but a few feet above the ground. Their repellor rays were relatively weak; just strong enough to lift them about ten or twelve feet from the surface. Hence they would draw but lightly upon the power broadcast from the city, and great numbers of them could be used. A special ray at the stern propelled them, and an extra-lift ray in the bow enabled them to nose up over ground

ch. ends next p.

obstacles. Their most formidable feature was the cone-shaped "canopy" of short-range disintegrator rays designed to spread down around them from a circular generator at the tip of a twenty-foot mast amidship. This would annihilate any projectile shot at it, for they naturally could not reach the ship without passing through the cone of rays.

It was instantly obvious that the groundships would prove to be the "tanks" of the 25th century, and with due allowance for the fact that they were protected with a sheathing of annihilating rays instead of with steel, that they would have about the same handicaps and advantages as tanks, except that since they would float lightly on short repellor rays, they could hardly resort to the destructive crushing tactics of the tanks of the First World War.

As soon as our first supplies of inertron-sheathed rockets came through, their invulnerability would be at an end, as indeed would be that of the Han cities themselves. But these projectiles were not yet out of the factories.

In the meantime, however, the groundships would be hard to handle. Each of them we understood would be equipped with a thin long-range dis-ray, mounted in a turret at the base of the mast.

We had no information as to the probable tactics of the Hans in the use of these ships. One sure method of destroying them would be to bury mines in their path, too deep for the penetration of their protecting canopy, which would not, our engineers estimated, cut deeper than about three feet a second. But we couldn't ring Nu-Yok with a continuous mine on a radius of from five to fifteen or twenty miles. Nor could we be certain beforehand of the direction of their attack.

In the end, after several hours' discussion, we agreed on a flexible defense. Rather than risk many lives, we would withdraw before them, test their effectiveness and familiarize ourselves with the tactics they adopted. If possible, we would send engineers in behind them from the flanks, to lay mines in the probable path of their return, providing their first attack proved to be a raid and not an advance to consolidate new positions.

3

WE SINK THE GROUNDSHIPS

Boss Handan, of the Winslows, a giant of a man, a two-fisted fighter and a leader of great sagacity,[1] had been selected by the council as our Boss *pro tem*,[2] and having given the scatter signal to the council, he retired to our general headquarters, which we had established on Second Mountain a few miles in the rear of the fighting front in a deep ravine.

There, in quarters cut far below the surface, he would observe every detail of the battle on the wonderful system of viewplates our ultrono engineers had constructed through a series of relays from ultroscope observation posts and individual cameramen.

Two hours before dawn our long distance scopemen reported a squadron of groundships leaving the enemy's disintegrator wall, and heading rapidly somewhat to the south of us, toward the site of the ancient city of Newark. The ultroscopes could detect no canopy operation. This in itself was not significant, for they were penetrating hills in their lines of vision, most of them, which of course blurred their pictures to a slight extent. But by now we had

---

[1] The quality of being sagacious (having or showing keen mental discernment and good judgment; shrewd).

[2] A Latin phrase meaning: for the time being.

a well-equipped electronoscope division, with instruments nearly equal to those of the Hans themselves; and these could detect no evidence of dis-rays in operation.

Handan appreciated our opportunity instantly, for no sooner had the import of the message on the Bosses' channel become clear than we heard his personal command snapped out over the long-gunners' general channel.

Nine hundred and seventy long-gunners on the south and west sides of the city, concealed in the dark fastnesses of the forests and hillsides, leaped to their guns, switched on their dial lights, and flipped the little lever combinations on their pieces that automatically registered them on the predetermined position of map section HM-243-839, setting their magazines for twenty shots, and pressing their fire buttons.

For what seemed an interminable instant nothing happened.

Then several miles to the southeast, an entire section of the country literally blew up in a fiery eruption that shot a mile into the air. The concussion, when it reached me, was terrific. The light was blinding.

And our scopemen reported the instant annihilation of the squadron.

What happened, of course, was this; the Hans knew nothing of our ability to see at night through our ultroscopes. Regarding itself as invisible in the darkness, and believing our instruments would pick up its location when its dis-rays went into operation, the squadron made the fatal error of not turning on its canopies.

To say that consternation overwhelmed the Han high command would be putting it mildly. Despite their use of code and other protective expedients, we picked up enough of their messages to know that the incident badly demoralized them.

Their next attempt was made in daylight. I was aloft in my swooper at the time, hanging motionless about a mile up. Below, the groundships looked like a number of oval lozenges gliding across a map, each surrounded by a circular halo of luminescence that was its dis-ray canopy.

They had nosed up over the spiny ridge of what once had been

Jersey City, and were moving across the meadowlands. There were twenty of them.

Coming to the darker green that marked the forest on the "map" below me, they adopted a wedge formation, and playing their pencil rays ahead of them, they began to beam a path for themselves through the forest. In my ears sounded the ultrophone instructions of my executives to the long-gunners in the forest, and one by one I heard the girls report their rapid retirement with their guns and other inertron-lightened equipment. I located several of them with my scopes, with which I could, of course, focus through the leafy screen above them, and noted with satisfaction the unhurried speed of their movements.

On plowed the Han wedge, while my girls separated before it and retired to the sides. With a rapidity much greater than that of the ships themselves, the beams penetrated deeper and deeper into the forest, playing continuously in the same direction, literally melting their way through, as a stream of hot water might melt its way through a snow bank.

Then a curious thing happened. One of the ships near one wing of the wedge must have passed over unusually soft ground, or perhaps some irregularity in the control of its canopy generator caused it to dig deeper into the earth ahead of it, for it gave a sudden downward lurch, and on coming up out of it, swerved a bit to one side, its offense beam slicing full into the ship echeloned[3] to the left ahead of it. That ship, all but a few plates on one side, instantly vanished from sight. But the squadron could not stop. As soon as a ship stood still, its canopy ray playing continuously in one spot, the ground around it was annihilated to a continuously increasing depth. A couple of them tried it, but within a space of seconds, they had dug such deep holes around themselves that they had difficulty in climbing out. Their commanders, however, had the foresight to switch off their offense rays, and so damaged no more of their comrades.

I switched in with my ultrophone on Boss Handan's channel, intending to report my observation, but found that one of our swooper scouts, who, like myself, was hanging above the Hans,

[3] A formation of troops, ships, aircraft, or vehicles in parallel rows with the end of each row projecting further than the one in front.

ch. ends next p.

was ahead of me. Moreover, he was reporting a suddenly developed idea that resulted in the untimely end of the Hans' groundship threat.

"Those ships can't climb out of deep holes, Boss," he was saying excitedly. "Lay a big barrage against them—no, not on them—in front of them—always in front of them. Pull it back as they come on. But churn hell out of the ground in front of them! Get the rocketmen to make a penetrative time rocket. Shoot it into the ground in front of them, deep enough to be below their canopy ray, see, and detonate under them as they go over it!"

I heard Handan's roar of exultation as I switched off again to order a barrage from my Wyoming girls. Then I threw my rocket motor to full speed and shot off a mile to one side, and higher, for I knew that soon there would be a boiling eruption below.

No smoke interfered with my view of it, for our atomic explosive was smokeless in its action. A line of blinding, flashing fire appeared in front of the groundship wedge. The ships plowed with calm determination toward it, but it withdrew before them, not steadily, but jerkily intermittent, so that the ground became a series of gigantic humps, ridges, and shell holes. Into these the Han ships wallowed, plunging ponderously yet not daring to stop while their protective canopy rays played, not daring to shut off these active rays.

One overturned. Our observers reported it. The result was a hail of rocket shells directly on the squadron. These could not penetrate the canopies of the other ships, but the one which had turned turtle was blown to fragments.

The squadron attempted to change its course and dodge the barrier in front of it. But a new barrier of blazing detonations and churned earth appeared on its flanks. In a matter of minutes it was ringed around, thanks to the skill of our fire control.

One by one the wallowing ships plunged into holes from which they could not extricate themselves. One by one their canopy rays were shut off, or the ships somersaulted off the knolls on which they perched, as their canopies melted the ground away from around them. So one by one they were destroyed.

Thus the second ground sortie of the Hans was annihilated.

4

HAN ELECTRONO-RAY SCIENCE

At this period, the Hans of Nu-Yok had only one airship equipped with their new armored repellor ray, their latest defense against our tactics of shooting rockets into the repellor rays and letting the latter hurl them up against the ships. They had developed a new steel alloy of tremendous strength, which passed their rep-ray with ease, but was virtually impervious to our most powerful explosives. Their supplies of this alloy were limited, for it could be produced only in the Lo-Tan shops, for it was only there that they could develop the degree of electronic power necessary for its manufacture.

This ship shot out toward our lines just as the last of the ground-ships turned turtle[1] and was blown to pieces. As it approached, the rockets of our invisible and widely scattered gunners in the forest below began to explode beneath its rep-ray plates. The explosions caused the great ship to plunge and roll mightily, but otherwise did it no serious harm that I could see, for it was very heavily armored.

Occasionally, rockets fired directly at the ship would find their mark and tear gashes in its side and bottom plates, but these hits were few. The ship was high in the air, and a far more difficult target than were its rep-ray columns. To hit the latter, our gunners

[1] Chiefly of a boat, to turn turtle means to capsize or overturn.

had only to gauge their aim vertically. Range could be practically ignored, since the rep-ray at any point above two-thirds the distance from the earth to the ship would automatically hurl the rocket upward against the rep-ray plate.

As the ship sped toward us, rocking, plunging and recovering, it began to beam the forest below. It was equipped with a superbeam too, which cut a swathe nearly a hundred feet wide wherever it played.

With visions of many a life snuffed out below me, I surrendered to the impulse to stage a single-handed attack on this ship, feeling quite secure in my floating shell of inertron. I nosed up vertically, and rocketed for a position above the ship. Then as I climbed upward, as yet unobserved in my tiny craft that was scarcely larger than myself, I trained my telultroscope on the Han ship, focusing through to a view of its interior.

Much as I had imbibed of this generation's hatred for the Hans, I was forced to admire them for the completeness and efficiency of this marvelous craft of theirs.

Constantly twirling the controls of my scope to hold the focus, I examined its interior from nose to stern.

It may be of interest at this point to give the reader a layman's explanation of the electronic or ionic machinery of these ships, and of their general construction, for today the general public knows little of the particular application of the electronic laws which the Hans used, although the practical application of ultronics are well understood.

Back in the 20th century I had, like literally millions of others, dabbled a bit in "radio" as we called it then; the science of the Hans was simply the superdevelopment of "electricity," "radio," and "broadcasting."

It must be understood that this explanation of mine is not technically accurate, but only what might be termed an illustrative approximation.

The Hans' power stations used to broadcast three distinct *powers* simultaneously. Our engineers called them the *starter*, the *pullee*, and the *sub-disintegrator*. The last named had nothing to do with the operation of the ships, but was exclusively the *powerizer* of the disintegrator generators.

The *starter* was not unlike the "radio" broadcasts of the 20th century. It went out at a frequency of about 1,000 kilocycles, had an amperage of approximately zero, but a voltage of two billion. Properly amplified by the use of *inductostatic* batteries (a development of the principle underlying the earth induction compass applied to the control of static) this current energized the *"A" ionomagnetic* coils on the airships, large and sturdy affairs, which operated the *Attractoreflex Receivers*, which in turn "pulled in" the second broadcast power known as the *pullee*, absorbing it from every direction, literally exhausting it from surrounding space. The *pullee* came in at about a half-billion volts, but in very heavy amperage, proportional to the capacity of the receiver, and on a long wave—at audio frequency in fact. About half of this power reception ultimately actuated the repellor ray generators. The other half was used to energize the *"B" ionomagnetic* coils, peculiarly wound affairs, whose magnetic fields constituted the only means of insulating and controlling the circuits of the three *powers*.

The repellor ray generators, operating on this current, and in conjunction with *twin synchronizers* in the power broadcast plant, developed two rhythmically variable ether-ground circuits of opposite polarity. In the *"X"* circuit, the negative was grounded along an ultraviolet beam from the ship's rep-ray generator. The positive connection was through the ether to the *"X" synchronizer* in the power plant, whose opposite pole was grounded. The *"Y"* circuit traveled the same course, but in the opposite direction.

The rhythmic variables of these two opposing circuits, as nearly as I can understand it, in heterodyning,[2] created a powerful material "push" from the earth, up along the violet ray beam against the rep-ray generator and against the two synchronizers at the power plant.

[2] Combining high-frequency signals to produce a lower frequency.

ch. ends next p.

This push developed molecularly from the earth-mass-resultant to the generator, and at the same fractional distance from the rep-ray generator to the power plant.

The force exerted upward against the ship was, of course, highly concentrated, being confined to the path of the ultraviolet beam. Air or any material substance, coming within the indicated section of the beam, was thrown violently upward. The ships actually rode on columns of air thus forcefully up-thrown. Their "home berths" and "stations" were constructed with air pits beneath. When they rose from ordinary ground in open country, there was a vast upheaval of earth beneath their generators at the instant of take-off; this ceased as they got well above ground level.

Equal pressure to the lifting power of the generator was exerted against the synchronizers at the power plant, but this force, not being concentrated directionally along an ultraviolet beam, involved a practical problem only at points relatively close to the synchronizers.

Of course the synchronizers were automatically controlled by the operation of the generators, and only the two were needed for any number of ships drawing power from the station, providing their protection was rugged enough to stand the strain.

Actually, they were isolated in vast spherical steel chambers with thick walls, so that nothing but air pressure would be hurled against them, and this, of course, would be self-neutralizing, coming as it did from all directions.

The *sub-disintegrator power* reached the ships as an ordinary broadcast reception at a negligible amperage, but from one to 500 "quints" (quintillions)[3] voltage, controllable only by the fields of the *"B" ionomagnetic* coils. It had a wavelength of about ten meters. In the dis-ray generator, this wavelength was broken up into an almost unbelievably high frequency, and became a directionally

[3] A number equal to 1 followed by 18 zeros; 10^{18}.

controlled wave of an infinitesimal fraction of an inch. This wave-length, actually identical with the diameter of an electron, that is to say, being accurately "tuned" to an electron, disrupted the orbital paths and balanced pulsations of the electrons within the atom, so desynchronizing them as to destroy polarity balance of the atom and causing it to cease to exist as an atom. It was in this way that the ray reduced matter to "nothingness."

This destruction of the atom, and a limited power for its reconstruction under certain conditions, marked the utmost progress of the Han science.

5
AMERICAN ULTRONIC SCIENCE

Our own engineers, working in shielded laboratories far underground, had established such control over the "de-atomized" electrons as to dissect them in their turn into *sub-electrons*. Moreover, they had carried through the study of this "order" to the point where they finally "dissected" the *sub-electron* into its component *ultrons*, for the fundamental laws underlying these successive orders are not radically dissimilar. And as they progressed, they developed constructive as well as destructive practice. Hence the great triumphs of ultron and inertron, our two wonderful synthetic elements, built up from super-balanced and sub-balanced ultronic whorls,[1] through the *sub-electronic* order into the *atomic* and *molecular*.

Hence also, come our relatively simple and beautifully efficient ultrophones and ultroscopes, which in their phonic and visual operation penetrate obstacles of material, electronic and sub-electronic nature without let or hindrance, and with the consumption of but infinitesimal power.

Static disturbance, I should explain, is negligible in the sub-electronic order, and non-existent in the ultronic.

[1] A pattern of spirals or concentric circles.

The pioneer expeditions of our engineers into the ultronic order, I am told, necessitated the use of most elaborate, complicated, and delicate apparatus, as well as the expenditure of most costly power, but once established there, all necessary power is developed very simply from tiny batteries composed of thin plates of *metultron* and *katultron*. These two substances, developed synthetically in much the same manner as ordinary ultron, exhibit dual phenomena which for sake of illustration I may compare with certain of the phenomena of radioactivity. As radium is constantly giving off electronic emanations and changing its atomic structure thereby, so *katultron* is constantly giving off ultronic emanations, and so changing its *sub-electronic* form, while *metultron*, its complement, is constantly attracting and absorbing ultronic values, and so changing its *sub-electronic* nature in the opposite direction. Thin plates of these two substances, when placed properly in juxtaposition, with insulating plates of inertron between, constitute a battery which generates an ultronic current.

And it is a curious parallel that just as there were many mysteries connected with the nature of electricity in the 20th century (mysteries which, I might mention, never *have* been solved, notwithstanding our penetration into the "sub-" orders) so there are certain mysteries about the ultronic current. It will flow, for instance, through an ultron wire, from the *katultron* to the *metultron* plate, as electricity will flow through a copper wire. It will short circuit between the two plates if the inertron insulation is imperfect. When the insulation is perfect, however, and no ultron metallic circuit is complete, the "current" (apparently the same that would flow through the metallic circuit) is projected into space in an absolutely straight line from the *katultron* plate, and received from space by the *metultron* plate on the same line. This line is the theoretical straight line passing through the mass-center of each plate. The shapes and angles of the plates have nothing to do with it, except that the perpendicular distance of the plate edges from the mass-center line determines thickness of the beam of parallel current-rays.

Thus a simple battery may be used either as a sender or receiver of current. Two batteries adjusted to the same center line become connected in series just as if they were connected by ultron wires.

In actual practice, however, two types of batteries are used; both the *foco* batteries and *broadcast* batteries.

Foco batteries are twin batteries, arranged to shoot a positive and a negative beam in the same direction. When these beams are made intermittent at light frequencies (though they are not light waves, nor of the same order as light waves) and are brought together, or focused, at a given spot, the space in which they cross radiates alternating ultronic current in every direction. This radiated *ultralight* acts like true light so long as the crossing beams vibrate at light frequencies, except in three respects: first, it is not visible to the eye; second, its "color" is exclusively dependent on the frequency of the *foco* beams, which determine the frequency of the alternating radiation. Material surfaces, it would appear, reflect them all in equal value, and the color of the resultant picture depends on the color of the *foco* frequencies. By altering these, a reddish, yellowish or bluish picture may be seen. In actual practice an orthochromatic mixture of frequencies is used to give a black, gray, and white picture. The third difference is this: rays pulsating in-line toward any ultron object connected with the rear plates of the twin batteries through rectifiers cannot be reflected by material objects, for it appears they are subject to a kind of "pull" which draws them straight through material objects, which in a sense are "magnetized" and while in this state offer no resistance.

Ultron, when so connected with battery terminals, glows with true light under the impact of *ultralight*, and if in the form of a lens or set of lenses, may be made to deliver a picture in any telescopic degree desired.

The essential parts of an ultroscope, then, are twin batteries

ch. ends next p.

with focal control and frequency control; an ultron shield, battery connected and adjustable, to intercept the direct rays from the *glow-spot*, with an ordinary light-shield between it and the lens; and the lens itself, battery connected and with more or less telescopic elaboration.

To look through a substance at an object, one has only to focus the *glow-spot* beyond the substance, but on the near side of the object and slightly above it.

A complete apparatus may be "set" for *penetrative, distance*, and *normal vision*.

In the first, which one would use to look through the forest screen from the air, or in examining the interior of a Han ship or any opaque structure, the *glow-spot* is brought low, at only a tiny angle above the vision line, and the shield, of course, must be very carefully adjusted.

Distance setting would be used, for instance, in surveying a valley beyond a hill or mountain; the *glow-spot* is thrown high to illuminate the entire scene.

In the *normal* setting, the *foco* rays are brought together close overhead and illuminate the scene just as a lamp of super brilliancy would in the same position.

For phonic communication, a spherical sending battery is a ball of *metultron*, surrounded by an insulating shell of inertron, and this in turn by a spherical shell of *katultron*, from which the current radiates in every direction, tuning being accomplished by frequency of intermissions, with audio-frequency modulation. The receiving battery has a core pole of *katultron* and an outer shell of *metultron*. The receiving battery, of course, picks up all frequencies, the undesired ones being tuned out in detection.

Tuning, however, is only a convenience for privacy and elimination of interference in ultrophonic communication. It is not involved as a necessity, for untuned currents may be broadcast at voice-controlled frequencies, directly and without any carrier wave.

To use plate batteries or single center-line batteries for phonic communication would require absolutely accurate directional aligning of sender and receiver, a very great practical difficulty, except when sender and receiver are relatively close and mutually visible.

This, however, is the regular system used in the Inter-Gang network for official communication. The senders and receivers used in this system are set only with the greatest difficulty, and by the aid of the finest laboratory apparatus, but once set, they are permanently locked in position at the stations, and barring earthquakes or insecure foundations, need no subsequent adjustment. Accuracy of alignment permits beam paths no thicker than the old lead pencils I used to use in the 20th century.

The non-interference of such communication lines, and the difficulty of cutting in on them from any point except immediately adjacent to the sender or receiver, is strikingly apparent when it is realized that every square inch of an imaginary plane bisecting the unlocated beam would have to be explored with a receiving battery in order to locate the beam itself.

A practical compromise between the spherical or universal broadcast senders and receivers on the one hand, and the single line batteries on the other, is the *multi-facet battery*. Another, and more practical device particularly for distance work, is the *window-spherical*. It is merely an ordinary spherical battery with a shielding shell with an opening of any desired size, from which a directionally controlled beam may be emitted in different forms, usually that simply of an expanding cone, with an angle of expansion sufficient to cover the desired territory at the desired point of reception.

AN UNEQUAL DUEL

But to return to my narrative, and my swooper, from which I was gazing at the interior of the Han ship.

This ship was not unlike the great dirigibles[1] of the 20th century in shape, except that it had no suspended control car nor gondolas, no propellers, and no rudders, aside from a permanently fixed double-fishtail stabilizer at the rear, and a number of "keels" so arranged as to make the most of the repellor ray airlift columns.

Its width was probably twice as great as its depth, and its length about twice its width. That is to say, it was about 100 feet from the main keel to the top-deck at their maximum distance from each other, about 200 feet wide amidship,[2] and between 400 and 500 feet long. It had in addition to the top-deck, three interior decks. In its general curvature the ship was a compromise between a true streamline design and a flattened cylinder.

For a distance of probably 75 to 100 feet back of the nose there were no decks except that formed by the bottom of the hull. But from this point back the decks ran to within a few feet of the stern.

At various spots on the hull curvature in this great "hollow nose"

[1] Airships capable of being steered, guided, or directed.
[2] The middle of a ship, longitudinally or laterally.

were platforms from which the crews of the dis-ray generators and the electronoscope and electronophone devices manipulated their apparatus.

Into this space from the forward end of the center deck, projected the control room. The walls, ceiling, and floor of this compartment were simply the surfaces of viewplates. There were no windows or other openings.

The operation officers within the control room, so far as their vision was concerned, might have imagined themselves suspended in space, except for the transmitters, levers and other signaling devices around them.

Five officers, I understand, had their posts in the control room; the captain, and the chiefs of *scopes*, *phones*, *dis-rays*, and *navigation*. Each of these was in continuous interphone communication with his subordinates in other posts throughout the ship. Each viewplate had its phone connecting with its "eye machines" on the hull, the crews of which would switch from telescopic to normal view at command.

There were, of course, many other viewplates at executive posts throughout the ship.

The Hans followed a peculiar system in the command of their ships. Each ship had a double complement[3] of officers. Active Officers and Base Officers. The former were in actual, active charge of the ship and its apparatus. The latter remained at the ship base, at desks equipped with viewplates and phones, in constant communication with their "correspondents" on the ship. They acted continuously as consultants, observers, recorders, and advisors during the flight or action. Although not primarily accountable for the operation of the ship, they were senior to, and in a sense responsible for the training and efficiency of the Active Officers.

The *ionomagnetic coils*, which served as the casings, "plates" and

[3] The number of people required to crew a ship.

insulators of the gigantic condensers, were all located amidship on a center line, reaching clear through from the top to the bottom of the hull, and reaching from the forward to the rear rep-ray generators; that is, from points about 110 feet from bow and stern. The crew's quarters were arranged on both sides of the coils. To the outside of these, where the several decks touched the hull, were located the various pieces of *phone, scope,* and *dis-ray* apparatus.

The ship into which I was gazing with my ultroscope (at a telescopic and penetrative setting), carried a crew of perhaps 150 men all told. And except for the strained looks on their evil yellow faces I might have been tempted to believe I was looking on some 25th century pleasure excursion, for there was no running around nor appearance of activity.

The Hans loved their ease, and despite the fact that this was a warship, every machine and apparatus in it was equipped with a complement of seats and specially designed couches, in which officers and men reclined as they gazed at their viewplates, and manipulated the little sets of controls placed convenient to their hands.

The picture was a comic one to me, and I laughed, wondering how such soft creatures had held the sturdy and virile American race in complete subjection for centuries. But my laugh died as my mind grasped at the obvious explanation. These Hans were only soft physically. Mentally they were hard, efficient, ruthless, and conscienceless.

Impulsively, I nosed my swooper down toward the ship and shot toward it at full rocket power. I had acted so swiftly that I had covered nearly half the distance toward the ship before my mind slowly drifted out of the daze of my emotion. This proved my undoing. Their scopeman saw me too quickly, for in heading directly at them I became easily visible, appearing as a steady, expanding point. Looking through their hull, I saw the crew of a dis-ray

ch. ends next p.

generator come suddenly to attention. A second later their beam engulfed me.

For an instant my heart stood still. But the inertron shell of my swooper was impervious to the disintegrator ray. I was out of luck, however, so far as my control over my tiny ship was concerned. I had been hurtling in a direct line toward the ship when the beam found me. Now, when I tried to swerve out of the beam, the swooper responded but sluggishly to the shift I made in the rocket angle. I was, of course, traveling straight down a beam of vacuum. As my craft slowly nosed to the edge of the beam, the air rushing into this vacuum from all sides threw it back in again.

Had I shot my ship across one of these beams at right angles, my momentum would have carried me through with no difficulty. But I had no momentum now except in the line of the beam, and this being a vacuum now, my momentum, under full rocket power, was vastly increased. This realization gave me a second and more acute thrill. Would I be able to check my little craft in time, or would I, helpless as a bullet itself, crash through the shell of the Han ship to my own destruction?

I shut off my rocketmotor, but noticed no practical diminution of speed.

It was the fear of the Hans themselves that saved me. Through my ultroscope I saw sudden alarm on their faces, hesitation, a frantic officer in the control room jabbering into his phone. Then shakily the crew flipped their beam off to the side. The jar on my craft was terrific. Its nose caught the rushing tumble of air first, of course, and my tail sailing in a vacuum, swung around with a sickening wrench. My swooper might as well have been a barrel in the tumult of waters at the foot of Niagara. What was worse, the Hans kept me in that condition. Three of their beams were now playing in my direction, but not directly on me except for split seconds. Their technique was to play their beams around me more than on me, jerking them this way and that, so as to form vacuum pockets into which the air slapped and roared as the beams shifted, tossing me around like a chip.

Desperately I tried to bring my craft under control, to point its nose toward the Han ship and discharge an explosive rocket. Bitterly I cursed my self-confidence, and my impulsive action. An experienced pilot of the present age would have known better than to be caught shooting straight down a dis-ray beam. He would have kept his ship shooting constantly at some angle to it, so that his momentum would carry him across it if he hit it. Too late I realized that there was more to the business of air fighting, than instinctive skill in guiding a swooper.

At last, when for a fraction of a second my nose pointed toward the Hans, I pressed the button of my rocket gun. I registered a hit, but not an accurate one. My projectile grazed an upper section of the ship's hull. At that it did terrific damage. The explosion battered in a section about fifty feet in diameter, partially destroying the top-deck.

At the same instant I had shot my rocket, I had, in a desperate attempt to escape that turmoil of tumbling air, released a catch and dropped all that it was possible to drop of my ultron ballast. My swooper shot upward, like a bubble streaking for the surface of water.

I was free of the trap in which I had been caught, but unable to take advantage of the confusion which reigned on the Han ship.

I was as helpless to maneuver my ship now, in its up-rush, as when I had been tumbling in the air pockets. Moreover, I was badly battered from plunging around in my shell like a pellet in a box, and partially unconscious.

I was miles in the air when I recovered myself. The swooper was steady enough now, but still rising, my instruments told me, and traveling in a general westward direction at full speed. Far below me was a sea of clouds, stretching from horizon to horizon, and through occasional breaks in its surface I could see still other seas of clouds at lower levels.

7

CAPTURED!

Certainly my situation was no less desperate. Unless I could find some method of compensating for my lost ballast, the inverse gravity of my inertron ship would hurl me continuously upward until I shot forth from the last air layer into space. I thought of jumping, and floating down on my inertron belt, but I was already too high for this. The air was too rarefied to permit breathing outside, though my little air compressors were automatically maintaining the proper density within the shell. If I could compress a sufficiently large quantity of air inside the craft, I would add to its weight, but there seemed little chance that I would myself be able to withstand sufficient compression.

I thought of releasing my inertron belt, but doubted whether this would be enough. Besides I might need the belt badly if I did find some method of bringing the little ship down, and it came too fast.

At last a plan came into my half-numbed brain that had some promise of success, though it was desperate enough. Cutting one of the hose pipes on my air compressor, and grasping it between my lips, I set to work to saw off the heads of the rivets that held the entire nose section of the swooper (inertron plates had to be grooved and riveted together, since the substance was impervious to heat and could not be welded). Desperately I sawed, hammered, and chiseled, until at last with a wrench and a snap, the plate broke away.

The released nose of the ship shot upward. The rest began to drop with me. How fast I dropped I do not know, for my instruments went with the nose. Half fainting, I grimly clenched the rubber hose between my teeth, while the little compressor "carried on" nobly, despite the wrecked condition of the ship, giving me just enough air to keep my lungs from collapsing.

At last I shot through a cloud layer, and a long time afterward, it seemed, another. From the way in which they flashed up to meet me and to appear away above me, I must have been dropping like a stone.

At last I tried the rocket motor, very gently, to check my fall. The swooper was, of course, dropping tail first, and I had to be careful lest it turn over with a sharp blast from the motor, and dump me out.

Passing through the third layer of clouds I saw the earth beneath me. Then I jumped, pulling myself up through the jagged opening, and leaping upward while the remains of my ship shot away below me.

On approaching the ground I opened my chute-cape, to further check my fall, and landed lightly, with no further mishap. Whereupon I promptly threw myself down and slept, so exhausted was I with my experience.

It was not until the next morning that I awoke and gazed about me. I had come down in mountainous country. My intention was to get my bearing by tuning in headquarters with my ultrophone. But to my dismay I found the little battery disks had been torn from the earflaps of my helmet, though my chest-disk transmitter was still in place, and so far as I could see, in working order. I could report my experience, but could receive no reply.

I spent a half hour repeating my story and explanation on the headquarters channel, then once more surveyed my surroundings, trying to determine in which direction I had better leap. Then there came a stab of pain on the top of my head, and I dropped unconscious.

I regained consciousness to find myself, much to my surprise, a prisoner in the hands of a foot detachment of some thirty Hans. My surprise was a double one: first, that they had not killed me instantly; second, that a detachment of them should be roaming this wild country afoot, obviously far from any of their cities, and with no ship hanging in the sky above them.

As I sat up, their officer grunted with satisfaction and growled a guttural command. I was seized and pulled roughly to my feet by four soldiers, and hustled along with the party into a wooded ravine, through which we climbed sharply upward. I surmised, correctly as it turned out, that some projectile had grazed my head, and I was in such shape that if it had not been for the fact that my inertron belt bore most of my weight, they would have had to carry me. But as it was I made out well, and at the end of an hour's climb was beginning to feel like myself again, though the Han soldiers around me were puffing and drooping as men will, no matter how healthy, when they are totally unaccustomed to physical effort.

At length the party halted for a rest. I observed them curiously. Except for a few brief exciting moments at the time of our air raid on the intelligence office in Nu-Yok, I had seen no living specimens of this yellow race at close quarters.

They looked little like the Mongolians of the 20th century, except for their slant eyes and round heads. The characteristic of the high cheek bones appeared to have been bred out of them, as were those of the relatively short legs and the muddy yellow skin. To call them yellow was more figurative than literal. Their skins were whiter than those of our own weather-tanned forest men. Nevertheless, their pigmentation was peculiar, and what there was of it looked more like a pale orange tint than the ruddiness of the Caucasian.

ch. ends p. 128

They were well formed, but rather undersized and soft-looking, small-muscled, and smooth-skinned, like young girls. Their features were finely chiseled, eyes beady, and nose slightly aquiline.

They were uniformed, not in close-fitting green or other shades of protective coloring, such as the unobtrusive gray of the Jersey Beaches or the leadened russet of the autumn uniforms of our people. Instead they wore loose fitting jackets of some silky material, and loose knee pants. This particular command had been equipped with form-molded boots of some soft material that reached above the knee under their pants. They wore circular hats with small crowns and wide rims. Their loose jackets were belted at the waist, and they carried for weapons each man a knife, a short double-edged sword, and what I took to be a form of magazine rocket gun. It was a rather bulky affair, short-barreled, and with a pistol grip. It was obviously intended to be fired either from the waist position or from some sort of support, like the old machine guns. It looked, in fact, like a rather small edition of the 20th century arm.

And have I mentioned the color of their uniforms? Their circular hats and pants were a bright yellow; their coats a flaming scarlet. What targets they were!

I must have chuckled audibly at the thought, for their commander who was seated on a folding stool one of his men had placed for him, glanced in my direction, and, at his arrogant gesture of command, I was prodded to my feet, and with my hands still bound, as they had been from the moment I recovered consciousness, I was dragged before him.

Then I knew what it was about these Hans that kept me in a turmoil of irritation. It was their sardonic, mocking, cruel smiles; smiles which left their stamp on their faces, even in repose. Now the commander was smiling tauntingly at me. When he spoke, it was in my own language.

"So!" he sneered. "You beasts have learned to laugh. You have gotten out of control in the last year or so. But that shall be remedied. In the meantime, a simple little surgical operation would make your smile a permanent one, reaching from ear to ear. But there, my orders are to deliver you and your equipment, all we have of it, intact. The Heaven-Born has had a whim."

"And who," I asked, "is this Heaven-Born?"

"San-Lan," he replied, "misbegotten spawn of the late High Priestess Nlui-Mok, and now Most Glorious Air Lord of All the Hans." He rolled out these titles with a bow of exaggerated respect toward the west, and in a tone of mockery. Those of his men who were near enough to hear, snickered and giggled.

I was to learn that this amazing attitude of his was typical rather than exceptional. Strange as it may seem, no Han rendered any respect to another, nor expected it in return; that is, not genuine respect. Their discipline was rigid and cold-bloodedly heartless. The most elaborate courtesies were demanded and accorded among equals and from inferiors to superiors, but such was the intelligence and moral degradation of this remarkable race, that every one of them recognized these courtesies for what they were; they must of necessity have been hollow mockeries. They took pleasure in forcing one another to go through with them, each trying to outdo the other in cynical, sardonic thrusts, clothed in the most meticulously ceremonious courtesy. As a matter of fact, my captor, by this crude reference to the origin of his ruler, was merely proving himself a crude fellow, guilty of a vulgarity rather than of a treasonable or disrespectful remark. An officer of higher rank and better breeding would have managed a clever innuendo, less direct, but equally plain.

I was about to ask him what part of the country we were in and where I was to be taken, when one of his men came running to him with a little portable electronophone, which he placed before him, with much bowing and scraping.

ch. ends next p.

He conversed through this for a while, and then condescended to give me the information that a ship would soon be above us, and that I was to be transferred to it. In telling me this, he managed to convey, with crude attempts at mock-courtesy, that he and his men would feel relieved to be rid of me as a menace to health and sanitation, and would take exquisite joy in inflicting me upon the crew of the ship.

8

HYPNOTIC TORTURE

Some twenty minutes later the ship arrived. It settled down slowly into the ravine on its repellor rays until it was but a few feet above the treetops. There it was stopped, and floated steadily, while a little cage was let down on a wire. Into this I was hustled and locked, whereupon the cage rose swiftly again to a hole in the bottom of the hull, into which it fitted snugly, and I stepped into the interior of a craft not unlike the one with which I had had my fateful encounter, the cage being unlocked.

The cabin in which I was confined was not an outside compartment, but was equipped with a number of viewplates.

The ship rose to a great height, and headed westward at such speed that the hum of the air past its smooth plates rose to a shrill, almost inaudible moan. After a lapse of some hours we came in sight of an impressive mountain range, which I correctly guessed to be the Rockies. Swerving slightly, we headed down toward one of the topmost pinnacles of the range, and there unfolded in one of the viewplates in my cabin a glorious view of Lo-Tan, the Magnificent, a fairy city of glistening glass spires and iridescent colors, piled up on sheer walls of brilliant blue, on the very tip of this peak.

Nor was there any sheen of shimmering disintegrator rays

surrounding it, to interfere with the sparkling sight. So far-flung were the defenses of Lo-Tan, I found, that it was considered impossible for an American rocket gunner to get within effective range, and so numerous were the dis-ray batteries on the mountain peaks and in the ravines, in this encircling line of defenses, drawn on a radius of no less than 100 miles, that even the largest craft, in the opinion of the Hans, could easily be brought to earth through air-pocketing tactics. And this, I was the more ready to believe after my own recent experience.

I spent two months as a prisoner in Lo-Tan. I can honestly say that during that entire time every attention was paid to my physical comfort. Luxuries were showered upon me. But I was almost continuously subjected to some form of mental torture or moral assault. Most elaborately staged attempts at seduction were made upon me with drugs, with women. Hypnotism was resorted to. Viewplates were faked to picture to me the complete rout[1] of American forces all over the continent. With incredible patience, and laboring under great handicaps, in view of the vigor of the American offensive, the Han intelligence department dug up the fact that somewhere in the forces surrounding Nu-Yok, I had left behind me Wilma, my bride of less than a year. In some manner, I will never tell how, they discovered some likeness of her, and faked an electronoscopic picture of her in the hands of torturers in Nu-Yok, in which she was shown holding out her arms piteously toward me, as though begging me to save her by surrender.

Surrender of what? Strangely enough, they never indicated that to me directly, and to this day I do not know precisely what they expected or hoped to get out of me. I surmise that it was information regarding the American sciences.

There was, however, something about the picture of Wilma in the hands of the torturers that did not seem real to me, and my

---

[1] Defeat.

mind still resisted. I remember gazing with staring eyes at that picture, the sweat pouring down my face, searching eagerly for some visible evidence of fraud and being unable to find it. It was the identical likeness of Wilma. Perhaps had my love for her been less great, I would have succumbed. But all the while I knew subconsciously that this was not Wilma. Product of the utmost of nobility in this modern virile, rugged American race, she would have died under even worse torture than these vicious Han scientists knew how to inflict, before she would have pleaded with me this way to betray my race and her honor.

But these were things that not even the most skilled of the Han hypnotists and psychoanalysts could drag from me. Their intelligence division also failed to pick up the fact that I was myself the product of the 20th century and not the 25th. Had they done so, it might have made a difference. I have no doubt that some of their most subtle mental assaults missed fire because of my own 20th century "denseness." Their hypnotists inflicted many horrifying nightmares on me, and made me do and say many things that I would not have done in my right senses. But even in the 20th century we had learned that hypnotism cannot make a person violate his fundamental concepts of morality against his will, and steadfastly I steeled my will against them.

I have since thought that I was greatly aided by my newness to this age. I have never, as a matter of fact, become entirely attuned to it. And even today I confess to a longing wish that man might travel backward as well as forward in time. Now that my Wilma has been at rest these many years, I wish that I might go back to the year 1927, and take up my old life where I left it off, in the abandoned mine near Scranton.

And at the period of which I speak, I was less attuned than now to the modern world. Real as my life was, and my love for my wife, there was much about it all that was like a dream, and in the midst of my tortures by the Hans, this complex—this habit of many

ch. ends p. 134

months—helped me to tell myself that this, too, was all a dream, that I must not succumb, for I would wake up in a moment.

And so they failed.

More than that, I think I won something nearer to genuine respect from those around me than any other Hans of that generation accorded to anybody.

Among these was San-Lan himself, the ruler. In the end it was he who ordered the cessation of these tortures, and quite frankly admitted to me his conviction that they had been futile and that I was in many senses a super-man. Instead of having me executed, he continued to shower luxuries and attentions on me, and frequently commanded my attendance upon him.

Another was his favorite concubine, Ngo-Lan, a creature of the most alluring beauty; young, graceful, and most delicately seductive, whose skill in the arts and sciences put many of their doctors to shame. This creature, his most prized possession, San-Lan with the utmost moral callousness ordered to seduce me, urging her to apply without stint and to its fullest extent, her knowledge of evil arts. Had I not seen the naked horror of her soul, that she let creep into her eyes for just one unguarded instant, and had it not been for my conviction of Wilma's faith in me, I do not know what—but suffice it to say that I resisted this assault also.

Had San-Lan only known it, he might have had a better chance of breaking down my resistance through another bit of femininity in his household, the little nine-year-old Princess Lu-Yan, his daughter.

I think San-Lan held something of real affection for this sprightly little mite, who in spite of the sickening knowledge of rottenness she had already acquired at this early age, was the nearest thing to innocence I found in Lo-Tan. But he did not realize this, and could not; for even the most natural and fundamental affection of the human race, that of parents for their offspring, had been so degraded and suppressed in this vicious Han civilization as to be unrecognizable. Naturally San-Lan could not understand the nature of my pity for this poor child, nor the fact that it might have proved a weak spot in my armor. But had he done so, I truly believe he would have been ready to inflict degradation, torture, and even death upon her, to make me surrender the information he wanted.

Yet this man, perverted product of a morally degraded race, had about him something of true dignity; something of sincerity, in a warped, twisted way. There were times when he seemed to sense vaguely, gropingly, wonderingly, that he might have a soul.

The Han philosophy for centuries had not admitted the existence of souls. Its conception embraced nothing but electrons, protons, and molecules, and still was struggling desperately for some shred of evidence that thoughts, willpower, and consciousness of self were nothing but chemical reactions. However, it had gotten no further than the negative knowledge we had in the 20th century, that a sick body dulls consciousness of the material world, and that knowledge, which all mankind has had from the beginning of time, that a dead body means a departed consciousness. They had succeeded in producing, by synthesis, what appeared to be living tissues, and even animals of moderately complex structure and rudimentary brains, but they could not give these creatures the full complement of life's characteristics, nor raise the brains to more than mechanical control of muscular tissues.

It was my own opinion that they never could succeed in doing so. This opinion impressed San-Lan greatly. I had expected him to snort his disgust, as the extreme school of evolutionists would have done in the 20th century. But the idea was as new to him and the scientists of his court as Darwinism was to the late 19th and early 20th centuries. So it was received with much respect. Painfully and with enforced mental readjustments, they began a philosophical search for excuses and justifications for the idea.

All of this amused me greatly, for of course neither the newness nor the orthodoxy of a hypothesis will make it true if it is not true, nor untrue if it is true. Nor could the luck or willpower, with which I had resisted their hypnotists and psychoanalysts, make what might or might not be a universal fact one whit more or less of

ch. ends next p.

a fact than it really was. But the prestige I had gained among them, and the novelty of my expressed opinion carried much weight with them.

Yet, did not even brilliant scientists frequently exhibit the same lack of logic back in the 20th century? Did not the historians, the philosophers of ancient Greece and Rome show themselves to be the same shrewd observers as those of succeeding centuries, the same masters of the logical and slaves of the illogical?

After all, I reflected, man makes little progress within himself. Through succeeding generations he piles up those resources which he possesses outside of himself, the tools of his hands, and the warehouses of knowledge for his brain, whether they be parchment manuscripts, printed book, or electronorecordographs. For the rest he is born today, as in ancient Greece, with a blank brain, and struggles through to his grave, with a more or less beclouded understanding, and with distinct limitations to what we used to call his "think tank."

This particular reflection of mine proved unpopular with them, for it stabbed their vanity, and neither my prestige nor the novelty of the idea was sufficient salve. These Hans for centuries had believed and taught their children that they were a super-race, a race of destiny. Destined to Whom, for What, was not so clear to them; but nevertheless destined to "elevate" humanity to some sort of super-plane. Yet through these same centuries they had been busily engaged in the extermination of "weaklings," whom, by their very persecutions, they had turned into "super men," now rising in mighty wrath to destroy them; and in reducing themselves to the depths of softening vice and flabby moral fiber. Is it strange that they looked at me in amazed wonder when I laughed outright in the midst of some of their most serious speculations?

9

THE FALL OF NU-YOK

My position among the Hans, in this period, was a peculiar one. I was at once a closely guarded prisoner and an honored guest. San-Lan told me frankly that I would remain the latter only so long as I remained an object of serious study or mental diversion to himself or his court. I made bold to ask him what would be done with me when I ceased to be such.

"Naturally," he said, "you will be eliminated. What else? It takes the services of fifteen men altogether to guard you; and men, you understand, cannot be produced and developed in less than eighteen years." He meditated frowningly for a moment. "That, by the way, is something I must take up with the Birth and Educational Bureau. They must develop some method of speeding growth, even at the cost of mental development. With your wild forest men getting out of hand this way, we are going to need greater resources of population, and need them badly.

"But," he continued more lightly, "there seems to be no need for you to disturb yourself over the prospect at present. It is true you have been able to resist our psychoanalysts and hypnotists, and so have no value to us from the viewpoint of military information, but as a philosopher, you have proved interesting indeed."

He broke off to give his attention to a gorgeously uniformed official who suddenly appeared on the large viewplate that formed one wall of the apartment. So perfectly did this mechanism operate, that the man might have been in the room with us. He made a low obeisance,[1] then rose to his full height and looked at his ruler with malicious amusement.

"Heaven-Born," he said, "I have the exquisite pain of reporting bad news."

San-Lan gave him a scathing look. "It will be less unpleasant if I am not distracted by the sight of you while you report."

At this the man disappeared, and the viewplate once more presented its normal picture of the mountains north of Lo-Tan; but the voice continued:

"Heaven-Born, the Nu-Yok fleet has been destroyed, the city is in ruins, and the newly formed ground brigades, reduced to 10,000 men, have taken refuge in the hills of Ron-Dak (the Adirondacks) where they are being pressed hard by the tribesmen, who have surrounded them."

For an instant San-Lan sat as though paralyzed. Then he leaped to his feet, facing the viewplate.

"Let me see you!" he snarled. Instantly the mountain view disappeared and the Intelligence Officer appeared again, this time looking a little frightened.

"Where is Lui-Lok?" he shouted. "Cut him in on my north plate. The commander who loses his city dies by torture. Cut him in. Cut him in!"

"Heaven-Born, Lui-Lok committed suicide. He leaped into a ray, when the rockets of the tribesmen began to penetrate the ray-wall. Lip-Hung is in command of the survivors. We have just had a message from him. We could not understand all of it. Reception was very weak because he is operating with emergency apparatus on Bah-Flo power. The Nu-Yok power broadcast plant has been blown up. Lip-Hung begs for a rescue fleet."

San-Lan, his expression momentarily becoming more vicious, now was striding up and down the room, while the poor wretch in the viewplate, thoroughly scared at last, stood trembling.

[1] A gesture expressing deferential respect, such as a bow or curtsy.

"What!" shrieked the tyrant. "He begs a rescue. A rescue of what? Of 10,000 beaten men and nothing better than makeshift apparatus? No fleet? No city? I give him and his 10,000 to the tribesmen! They are of no use to us now! Get out! Vanish! No, wait! Have any of the beasts' rockets penetrated the ray-walls of other cities?"

"No, Heaven-Born, no. It is only at Nu-Yok that the tribesmen used rockets sheathed in the same mysterious substance they use on their little aircraft and which cannot be disintegrated by the ray." (He meant inertron, of course.)

San-Lan waved his hand in dismissal. The officer dissolved from view, and the mountains once more appeared, as though the whole side of the room were of glass.

More slowly he paced back and forth. He was the caged tiger now, his face seamed with hate and the desperation of foreshadowed doom.

"Driven out into the hills," he muttered to himself. "Not more than 10,000 of them left. Hunted like beasts—and by the very beasts we ourselves have hunted for centuries. Cursed be our ancestors for letting a single one of the spawn live!" He shook his clenched hands above his head. Then, suddenly remembering me, he turned and glared.

"Forest man, what have you to say?" he demanded.

Thus confronted, there stole over me that same detached feeling that possessed me the day I had been made Boss of the Wyomings.

"It is the end of the Air Lords of Han," I said quietly. "For five centuries command of the air has meant victory. But this is so no longer. For more than three centuries your great, gleaming cities have been impregnable in all their arrogant visibility. But that day is done also. Victory returns once more to the ground, to men invisible in the vast expanse of the forest which covers the ruins of the civilization destroyed by your ancestors. Ye have sown destruction. Ye shall reap it!

"Your ancestors thought they had made mere beasts of the American race. Physically you did reduce them to the state of beasts. But men do have souls, San-Lan, and in their souls the Americans still cherished the spark of manhood, of honor, of independence. While the Hans have degenerated into a race of sleek, pampered beasts

ch. ends p. 141

themselves, they have unwittingly bred a race of super-men out of those they sought to make animals. You have bred your own destruction. Your cities shall be blasted from their foundations. Your air fleets shall be brought crashing to earth. You have your choice of dying in the wreckage, or of fleeing to the forests, there to be hunted down and killed as you have sought to destroy us!"

And the ruler of all the Hans shrank back from my outstretched finger as though it had been in truth the finger of doom.

But only for a moment. Suddenly he snarled and crouched as though to spring at me with his bare hands. By a mighty convulsion of the will he regained control of himself, however, and assumed a manner of quiet dignity. He even smiled—a slow, crooked smile.

"No," he said, answering his own thought. "I will not have you killed now. You shall live on, my honored guest, to see with your own eyes how we shall exterminate your animal-brethren in their forests. With your own ears you shall hear their dying shrieks. The cold science of Han is superior to your spurious knowledge. We have been careless. To our cost we have let you develop brains of a sort. But we are still superior. We shall go down into the forests and meet you. We shall beat you in your own element. When you have seen and heard this happen, my Council shall devise for you a death by scientific torture, such as no man in the history of the world has been honored with."

I must digress here a bit from my own personal adventures to explain briefly how the fall of Nu-Yok came about, as I learned it afterward.

Upon my capture by the Hans, my wife, Wilma, courageously had assumed command of my Gang, the Wyomings.

Boss Handan, of the Winslows, who was directing the American forces investing Nu-Yok, contented himself for several weeks with maintaining our lines, while waiting for the completion of the first supply of inertron-jacketed rockets. At last they arrived with a limited quantity of very high-powered atomic shells, a trifle over a hundred of them to be exact. But this number, it was estimated, would be enough to reduce the city to ruins. The rockets were distributed, and the day for the final bombardment was set.

The Hans, however, upset Handan's plans by launching a ground expedition up the west bank of the Hudson. Under cover of an air raid to the southwest, in which the bulk of their ships took part, this ground expedition shot northward in low-flying ships.

The raiding air fleet plowed deep into our lines in their famous "cloud-bank" formation, with down-playing disintegrator rays so concentrated as to form a virtual curtain of destruction. It seared a scar path a mile and a half wide fifteen miles into our territory.

Everyone of our rocket gunners caught in this section was annihilated. Altogether we lost several hundred men and girls.

Gunners to each side of the raiding ships kept up a continuous fire on them. Most of the rockets were disintegrated, for Handan would not permit the use of the inertron rockets against the ships. But now and then one found its way through the playing beams, hit a repellor ray and was hurled up against a Han ship, bringing it crashing down.

The orders that Handan barked into his ultrophone were, of course, heard by every long-gunner in the ring of American forces around the city, and nearly all of them turned their fire on the Han airfleet, with the exception of those equipped with the inertron rockets.

These latter held to the original target and promptly cut loose on the city with a shower of destruction which the disintegrator-ray walls could not stop. The results produced awe even in our own ranks.

Where an instant before had stood the high-flung masses and towers of Nu-Yok, gleaming red, blue and gold in the brilliant sunlight, and shimmering through the iridescence of the ray "wall," there was a seething turmoil of gigantic explosions.

Surging billows of debris were hurled skyward on gigantic pulsations of blinding light, to the detonations that shook men from their feet in many sections of the American line seven and eight miles away.

As I have said, there were only some hundred of the inertron

ch. ends next p.

rockets among the Americans, long and slender, to fit the ordinary guns, but the atomic laboratories hidden beneath the forests, had outdone themselves in their construction. Their release of atomic force was nearly 100 percent, and each one of them was equal to many hundred tons of trinitrotoluene, which I had known in the First World War, five hundred years before, as "T.N.T."

It was all over in a few seconds. Nu-Yok had ceased to exist, and the waters of the bay and the rivers were pouring into the vast hole where a moment before had been the rocky strata beneath lower Manhattan.

Naturally, with the destruction of the city's power-broadcasting plant the Han air fleet had plunged to earth.

But the ships of the ground expedition up the river, hugging the treetops closely, had run the gauntlet of the American long-gunners who were busily shooting at the other Han fleet, high in the air to the southwest, and about half of them had landed before their ships were robbed of their power. The other half crashed, taking some 10,000 or 12,000 Han troops to destruction with them. But from those which had landed safely, emerged the 10,000 who now were the sole survivors of the city, and who took refuge in wooded fastnesses of the Adirondacks.

The Americans with their immensely greater mobility, due to their jumping belts and their familiarity with the forest, had them ringed in within twenty-four hours.

But owing to the speed of the maneuvers, the lines were not as tightly drawn as they might have been, and there was considerable scattering of both American and Han units. The Hans could make only the weakest short-range use of their newly developed disintegrator-ray field units, since they had only distant sources of power-broadcast on which to draw. On the other hand, the Americans could use their explosive rockets only sparingly for fear of hitting one another.

So the battle was finished in a series of desperate hand-to-hand encounters in the ravines and mountain slopes of the district.

The Mifflins and Altoonas, themselves from rocky, mountainous sections, gave a splendid account of themselves in this fighting, leaping to the craggy slopes above the Hans, and driving them down into the ravines, where they could safely concentrate on them the fire of depressed rocket guns.

The Susquannas, with their great inertron shields, which served them well against the weak rays of the Hans, pressed forward irresistibly every time they made contact with a Han unit, their short-range rocket guns sending a hail of explosive destruction before them.

But the Delawares, with their smaller shields, inertron leg-guards and helmets, and their ax-guns, made faster work of it. They would rush the Hans, shooting from their shields as they closed in, and finish the business with their ax-blades and the small rocket guns that formed the handles of their axes.

It was my own unit of Wyomings, equipped with bayonet guns not unlike the rifles of the First World War, that took the most terrible toll from the Hans.

They advanced at the double, laying a continuous barrage before them as they ran, closing with the enemy in great leaps, cutting, thrusting and slicing with those terrible double-ended weapons in a vicious efficiency against which the Hans with their swords, knives and spears were utterly helpless.

And so my prediction that the war would develop hand-to-hand fighting was verified at the outset.

None of the details of this battle of the Ron-Daks were ever known in Lo-Tan. Not more than the barest outlines of the destruction of the survivors of Nu-Yok were ever received by San-Lan and his Council. And of course, at that time I knew no more about it than they did.

10

LIFE IN LO-TAN, THE MAGNIFICENT

San-Lan's attitude toward me underwent a change. He did not seek my company as he had done before, and so those long discussions and mental duels in which we pitted our philosophies against each other came to an end. I was, I suspected, an unpleasant reminder to him of things he would rather forget, and my presence was an omen of impending doom. That he did not order my execution forthwith was due, I believe to a sort of fascination in me, as the personification of this (to him) strange and mysterious race of super-men who had so magically developed overnight from "beasts" of the forest.

But though I saw little of him after this, I remained a member of his household, if one may speak of a "household" where there is no semblance of house.

The imperial apartments were located at the very summit of the Imperial Tower, the topmost pinnacle of the city, itself clinging to the sides and peak of the highest mountain in that section of the Rockies. There were days when the city seemed to be built on a rugged island in the midst of a sea of fleecy whiteness, for frequently the cloud level was below the peak. And on such days the only visual communications with the world below was through the viewplates which formed nearly all the interior walls of the thousands of apartments (for the city was, in fact, one vast building) and upon which the tenants could tune in almost any views they wished from an elaborate system of public television and projectoscope broadcasts.

Every Han city had many public-view broadcasting stations, operating on tuning ranges which did not interfere with other communication systems. For slight additional fees a citizen in Lo-Tan might, if he felt so inclined, "visit" the seashore, or the lakes or the forests of any part of the country, for when such scene was thrown on the walls of an apartment, the effect was precisely the same as if one were gazing through a vast window at the scene itself.

It was possible too, for a slightly higher fee, to make a mutual connection between apartments in the same or different cities, so that a family in Lo-Tan, for instance, might "visit" friends in Fis-Ko (San Francisco) taking their apartment, so to speak, along with them; being to all intents and purposes separated from their "hosts" only by a big glass wall which interfered neither with vision nor conversation.

These public view and visitation projectoscopes explain that utter depth of laziness into which the Hans had been dragged by their civilization. There was no incentive for anyone to leave his apartment unless he was in the military or air service, or a member of one of the repair services which from time to time had to scoot through the corridors and shafts of the city, somewhat like the ancient fire departments, to make some emergency repair to the machinery of the city or its electrical devices.

Why should he leave his house? Food, wonderful synthetic concoctions of any desired flavor and consistency (and for additional fee conforming to the individual's dietary prescription) came to him through a shaft, from which his tray slid automatically on to a convenient shelf or table.

At will he could tune in a theatrical performance of talking pictures. He could visit and talk with his friends. He breathed the freshest of filtered air right in his own apartment, at any temperature he desired, fragrant with the scent of flowers, the aromatic smell of the pine forests or the salt tang of the sea, as he might prefer. He could "visit" his friends at will, and though his apartment actually might be buried many thousand feet from the outside wall of the city, it was none the less an "outside" one, by virtue of its viewplate walls. There was even a tube system with trunk, branch, and local lines and an automagnetic switching system, by which articles within certain size limits could be dispatched from an apartment to any other in the city.

The women actually moved about through the city more than the men, for they had no fixed duties. No work was required of them, and though nominally free, their dependence upon the government pension for their necessities and on their "husbands" (of the moment) for their luxuries, reduced them virtually to the condition of slaves.

Each had her own apartment in the Lower City, with but a single small viewplate, very limited "visitation" facilities, and a minimum credit for food and clothing. This apartment was assigned to her on graduation from the State School, in which she had been placed as an infant, and it remained hers so long as she lived, regardless of whether she occupied it or not. At the conclusion of her various "marriages" she would return there, pending her endeavors to make a new match. Naturally, as her years increased, her returns became more frequent and her stay of longer duration, until finally, abandoning hope of making another match, she finished out her days there, usually in drunkenness and whatever other forms of cheap dissipation she could afford on her dole,[1] starving herself.

Men also received the same State pension, sufficient for the necessities but not for the luxuries of life. They got it only as an old-age pension, and on application.

✻   ✻   ✻

When boys graduated from the State School they generally were "adopted" by their fathers and taken into the latter's households, where they enjoyed luxuries far in excess of their own earning power. It was not that their fathers wasted any affection on them,

[1] Regular relief payments to the unemployed distributed by a government.

for as I have explained before, the Hans were so morally atrophied and scientifically developed that love and affection, as we Americans knew them, were unexperienced or suppressed emotions with them. They were replaced by lust and pride of possession. So long as it pleased a father's vanity, and he did not miss the cost, he would keep a son with him, but no longer.

Young men, of course, started to work at the minimum wage, which was somewhat higher than the pension. There was work for everybody in positions of minor responsibility, but very little hard work.

Upon receiving his appointment from one or another of the big corporations which handled the production and distribution of the vast community (the shares of which were pooled and held by the government—that is, by San-Lan himself—in trust for all the workers, according to their positions) he would be assigned to an apartment-office, or an apartment adjoining the group of offices in which he was to have his desk. Most of the work was done in single apartment-offices.

The young man, for instance, might recline at his ease in his apartment near the top of the city, and for three or four hours a day inspect, through his viewplate and certain specially installed apparatus, the output of a certain process in one of the vast automatically controlled food factories buried far underground beneath the base of the mountain, where the moan of its whirring and throbbing machinery would not disturb the peace and quiet of the citizens on the mountain top. Or he might be required simply to watch the operation of an account machine in an automatic store.

There is no denying that the economic system of the Hans was marvelous. A suit of clothes, for instance, might be delivered in a man's apartment without a human hand having ever touched it.

Having decided that he wished a suit of a given general style, he would simply tune in a visual broadcast of the display of various selections, and when he had made his choice, dial the number of the item and press the order button. Simultaneously the charge would be automatically made against his account number, and credited as a sale on the automatic records of that particular factory in the account house. And his account plate, hidden behind a little wall door, would register his new credit balance. An automatically packaged suit that had been made to style and size-standard by automatic machinery from synthetically produced material, would slip into the delivery chute, magnetically addressed, and in anywhere from a few seconds to thirty minutes or so, according to the volume of business in the chutes, drop into the delivery basket in his room.

Daily his wages were credited to his account, and monthly his share of the dividends likewise (according to his position) from the Imperial Investment Trust, after deduction of taxes (through the automatic bookkeeping machines) for the support of the city's pensioners and whatever sum San-Lan himself had chosen to deduct for personal expenses and gratuities.

A man could not bequeath his ownership interest in industry to his son, for that interest ceased with his death, but his credit accumulation, on which interest was paid, was credited to his eldest recorded son as a matter of law.

Since many of these credit fortunes (The Hans had abandoned gold as a financial basis centuries before) were so big that they drew interest in excess of the utmost luxury costs of a single individual, there was a class of idle rich consisting of eldest sons, passing on these credit fortunes from generation to generation. But younger sons and women had no share in these fortunes, except by the whims and favor of the "Man-Dins" (Mandarins), as these inheritors were known.

These Man-Dins formed a distinct class of the population, and numbered about five percent of it. It was distinct from the Ku-Li (coolie) or common people, and from the "Ki-Ling" or aristocracy composed of those more energetic men (at least mentally more energetic) who were the active or retired executive heads of the various industrial, educational, military, or political administrations.

A man might, if he so chose, transfer part of his credit to a woman favorite, which then remained hers for life or until she used it up, and of course, the prime object of most women, whether as wives, or favorites, was to beguile a settlement of this sort out of some wealthy man.

When successful in this, and upon reassuming her freedom,

ch. ends p. 150

a woman ranked socially and economically with the Man-Dins. But on her death, whatever remained of her credit was transferred to the Imperial fund.

When one considers that the Hans, from the days of their exodus from Mongolia and their conquest of America, had never held any ideal of monogamy, and the fact that marriage was but a temporary formality which could be terminated on official notice by either party, and that after all it gave a woman no real rights or prerogatives that could not be terminated at the whim of her husband, and established her as nothing but the favorite of his harem, if he had an income large enough to keep one, or the most definitely acknowledged of his favorites if he hadn't, it is easy to see that no such thing as a real family life existed among them.

Free women roamed the corridors of the city, pathetically importuning marriage, and wives spent most of the time they were not under their husbands' watchful eyes in flirtatious attempts to provide themselves with better prospects for their next marriages.

Naturally the biggest problem of the community was that of stimulating the birth rate. The system of special credits to mothers had begun centuries before, but had not been very efficacious[2] until women had been deprived of all other earning power, and even at the time of which I write it was only partially successful, in spite of the heavy bounties for children. It was difficult to make the bounties sufficiently attractive to lure the women from their more remunerative light flirtations. Eugenic standards also were a handicap.

As a matter of fact, San-Lan had under consideration a revolutionary change in economic and moral standards, when the revolt of the forest men upset his delicately laid plans, for, as he had explained to me, it was no easy thing to upset the customs of centuries in what he was pleased to call the "morals" of his race.

[2] Effective.

He had another reason too. The physically active men of the community were beginning to acquire a rather dangerous domination. These included men in the army, in the airships, and in those relatively few civilian activities in which machines could not do the routine work and thinking. Already common soldiers and air crews demanded and received higher remuneration than all except the highest of the Ki-Ling, the industrial and scientific leaders, while mechanics and repairmen who could, and would, work hard physically, commanded higher incomes than Princes of the Blood, and though constituting only a fraction of one per cent of the population they actually dominated the city. San-Lan dared take no important step in the development of the industrial and military system without consulting their council or Yun-Yun (Union), as it was known.

Socially the Han cities were in a chaotic condition at this time, between morals that were not morals, families that were not families, marriages that were not marriages, children who knew no homes, work that was not work, eugenics that didn't work; Ku-Lis who envied the richer classes but were too lazy to reach out for the rewards freely offered for individual initiative; the intellectually active and physically lazy Ki-Lings who despised their lethargy; the Man-Din drones who regarded both classes with supercilious[3] toleration; the Princes of the Blood, arrogant in their assumption of a heritage from a Heaven in which they did not believe; and finally the three castes[4] of the army, air, and industrial repair services, equally arrogant and with more reason in their consciousness of physical power.

*   *   *

The army exercised a cruelly careless and impartial police power over all classes, including the airmen, when the latter were in port. But it did not dare to touch the repair men, who, so far as

[3] Arrogantly superior; showing contemptuous indifference.
[4] In this context: any class or group of people who inherit exclusive privileges or are perceived as socially distinct.

ch. ends next p.

I could ever make out, roamed the corridors of the city at will during their hours off duty, wreaking their wills on whomever they met, without let or hindrance.

Even a Prince of the Blood would withdraw into a side corridor with his escort of a score of men to let one of these labor "kings" pass, rather than risk an altercation which might result in trouble for the government with the Yun-Yun, regardless of the rights and wrongs of the case, unless a heavy credit transference was made from the balance of the Prince to that of the worker. For the machinery of the city could not continue in operation a fortnight, before some accident requiring delicate repair work would put it partially out of commission. And the Yun-Yun was quick to resent anything it could construe as a slight on one of its members.

In the last analysis it was these Yun-Yun men, numerically the smallest of the classes, who ruled the Han civilization, because for all practical purposes they controlled the machinery on which that civilization depended for its existence.

Politically, San-Lan could balance the organizations of the army and the air fleets against each other, but he could not break the grip of the repairmen on the machinery of the cities and the power broadcast plants.

11

THE FOREST MEN ATTACK

Many times during the months I remained prisoner among the Hans I had tried to develop a plan of escape, but could conceive of nothing which seemed to have any reasonable chance of success.

While I was allowed almost complete freedom within the confines of the city, and sometimes was permitted to visit even the military outposts and disintegrator ray batteries in the surrounding mountains, I was never without a guard of at least five men under the command of an officer. These men were picked soldiers, and they were armed with powerful though short-range disintegrator-ray pistols, capable of annihilating anything within a hundred feet. Their vigilance never relaxed. The officer on duty kept constantly at my side, or a couple of paces behind me, while certain of the others were under strict orders never to approach within my reach, nor to get more than forty feet away from me. The thought occurred to me once to seize the officer at my side and use him as a shield, until I found that the guard were under orders to destroy both of us in such a case.

So in this fashion I roamed the city corridors, wherever I wished. I visited the great factories at the bottom of the shafts that led to the base of the mountain, where, unattended by any mechanics, great turbines whirred and moaned, giant pistons plunged back and forth, and immense systems of chemical vats, piping and converters, automatically performed their functions with the assistance of no human hand, but under the minute television inspection of many perfumed dandies reclining at their ease before viewplates in their apartment offices in the city, that clung to the mountain peak far above.

There were just two restrictions on my freedom of movement. I was allowed nowhere near the power-broadcasting station on the peak, nor the complement of it which was buried three miles below the base of the mountain. And I was never allowed to approach within a hundred feet of any disintegrator ray machine when I visited the military outposts in the surrounding mountains.

I first noticed the "escape tunnels" one day when I had descended to the lowest level of all, the location of the Electronic Plant, where machines, known as "reverse disintegrators," fed with earth and crushed rock by automatic conveyors, subjected this material to the disintegrator ray, held the released electrons captive within their magnetic fields and slowly refashioned them into supplies of metals and other desired elements.

My attention was attracted to the tunnels by the unusual fact that men were busily entering and leaving them. Almost the entire repair force seemed to be concentrated here. Stocky, muscular men they were, with the same modified Oriental countenances as the rest of the Hans, but with a certain ruggedness about them that was lacking in the rest of the indolent[1] population. They sweated as they labored over the construction of magnetic cars evidently designed to travel down these tunnels, automatically laying pipe lines for ventilation and temperature control. The tunnels themselves appeared to have been driven with disintegrator rays, which could bore rapidly through the solid rock, forming glassy iridescent walls as they bored, and involving no problem of debris removal.

I asked San-Lan about it the next time I saw him, for the officer of my guard would give me no information.

The supreme ruler of the Hans smiled mockingly.

"There is no reason why you should not know their purpose,"

[1] Lazy.

he said, "for you will never be able to stop our use of them. These tunnels constitute the road to a new Han era. Your forest men have turned our cities into traps, but they have not trapped our minds and our powers over Nature. We are masters still; masters of the world, and of the forest men.

"You have revolutionized the tactics of warfare with your explosive rockets and your strategy of fighting from concealed positions, miles away, where we cannot find you with our beams. You have driven our ships from the air, and you may destroy our cities. But we shall be gone.

"Down these tunnels we shall depart to our new cities, deep under ground, and scattered far and wide through the mountains. They are nearly completed now.

"You will never blast us out of these, even with your most powerful explosives, because they will be more difficult for you to find than it is for us to locate a forest gunner somewhere beneath his leafy screen of miles of trees, and because they will be too far underground."

"But," I objected, "man cannot live and flourish like a mole continually removed from the light of day, without the health-giving rays of the sun, which man needs."

"No?" San-Lan jeered. "Wild tribesmen might not be able to, but we are a civilization. We shall make our own sunlight to order in the bowels of the earth. If necessary, we can manufacture our air synthetically; not the germ-laden air of Nature, but absolutely pure air. Our underground cities will be heated or refrigerated artificially as conditions may require. Why should we not live underground if we desire? We produce all our needs synthetically.

"Nor will you be able to locate our cities with electronic indicators.

"You see, Rogers, I know what is in your mind. Our scientists have planned carefully. All our machinery and processes will be shielded so that no electronic disturbances will exist at the surface.

"And then, from our underground cities we will emerge at leisure to wage merciless war on your wild men of the forest, until we have at last done what our forefathers should have done, exterminated them to the last beast."

ch. ends p. 156

He thrust his jeering face close to mine. "Have you any answer to that?" he demanded.

My impulse was to plant my fist in his face, for I could think of no other answer. But I controlled myself, and even forced a hearty laugh to irritate him.

"It is a fine plan," I admitted, "but you will not have time to carry it through. Long before you can complete your new cities you will have been destroyed."

"They will be completed within the week," he replied triumphantly. "We have not been asleep, and our mechanical and scientific resources make us masters of time as well as the earth. You shall see."

Naturally I was worried. I would have given much if I could have passed this information on to our chiefs.

But two days later a mighty exultation arose within me, when from far to the east and also to the south there came the rolling and continuous thunder of rocket fire. I was in my own apartment at the time. The Han captain of my guard was with me, as usual, and two guards stood just within the door. The others were in the corridor outside. And as soon as I heard it, I questioned my jailer with a look. He nodded assent, and I did what probably every disengaged person in Lo-Tan did at the same moment, tuned in on the local broadcast of the Military Headquarters View and Control Room.

It was as though the side wall of my apartment had dissolved, and we looked into a large room or office which had no walls or ceiling, these being replaced by the interior surface of a hemisphere, which was in fact a vast viewplate on which those in the room could see in every direction. Some 200 staff officers had their desks in this room. Each desk was equipped with a system of small viewplates of its own, and each officer was responsible for a given directional section of the "map," and busied himself with teleprojectoscope examination of it, quite independently of the general view thrown on the dome plate.

At a raised circular desk in the center, which was composed entirely of viewplates, sat the Executive Marshal, scanning the hemisphere, calling occasionally for telescopic views of one section or another on his desk plates, and noting the little pale green signal lights that flashed up as Sector Observers called for his attention.

Members of Strategy Board, Base Commanders of military units, and San-Lan himself, I understood, sat at similar desks in their private offices, on which all these views were duplicated, and in constant verbal and visual communication with one another and with the Executive Marshal.

The particular view which appeared on my own wall fortunately showed the east side of the dome viewplate and in one corner of my picture appeared the Executive Marshal himself.

Although I was getting a viewplate picture of a viewplate picture, I could see the broad, rugged valley to the east plainly, and the relatively low ridge beyond, which must have been some thirty miles away.

It was beyond this, evidently far beyond it, that the scene of the action was located, for nothing showed on the plate but a misty haze permeated by indefinite and continuous pulsations of light, and against which the low mountain ridge stood out in bold relief.

Somewhere on the floor of the Observation room, of course, was a Sector Observer who was looking beyond that ridge, probably through a projectoscope station in the second or third "circle," located perhaps on that ridge or beyond it.

At the very moment I was wishing for his facilities the Executive Marshal leaned over to a microphone and gave an order in a low tone. The hemispherical view dissolved, and another took its place, from the third circle. And the view was now that which would be seen by a man standing on the low distant ridge.

There was another broad valley, a wide and deep canyon, in fact, and beyond this still another ridge, the outlines of which were already beginning to fade into the on-creeping haze of the barrage. The flashes of the great detonating rockets were momentarily becoming more vivid.

"That's the Gok-Man ridge," mused the Han officer beside me in the apartment, "and the Forest Men must be more than fifty miles beyond that."

"How do you figure that?" I asked curiously.

"Because obviously they have not penetrated our scout lines.

ch. ends next p.

See that line of observers nearest the dome itself. They're all busy with their desk plates. They're in communication with the scout line. The scout line broadcast is still in operation. It looks as though the line is still unpierced, but the tribesmen's rockets are sailing over and falling this side of it."

All through the night the barrage continued. At times it seemed to creep closer and then recede again. Finally it withdrew, pulling back to the American lines, to alternately advance and recede. At last I went to sleep. The Han officer seemed to be a relatively good-natured fellow for one of his race, and he promised to awake me if anything further of interest took place.

He didn't though. When I awoke in the morning, he gave me a brief outline of what had happened.

It was pieced together from his own observations and the public news broadcast.

THE MYSTERIOUS AIR BALLS

The American barrage had been a long distance bombardment, designed, apparently, to draw the Han disintegrator ray batteries into operation and so reveal their positions on the mountain tops and slopes, for the Hans, after the destruction of Nu-Yok, had learned quickly that concealment of their positions was a better protection than a surrounding wall of disintegrator rays shooting up into the sky.

The Hans, however, had failed to reply with disintegrator rays. For already this arm, which formerly they had believed invincible, was being restricted to a limited number of their military units, and their factories were busy turning out explosive rockets not dissimilar to those of the Americans in their motive power and atomic detonation. They had replied with these, shooting them from unrevealed positions, and at the estimated positions of the Americans.

Since the Americans, not knowing the exact location of the Han outer line, had shot their barrage over it, and the Hans had fired at unknown American positions, this first exchange of fire had done little more than to churn up vast areas of mountain and valley.

The Hans appeared to be elated, to feel that they had driven off an American attack. I knew better. The next American move, I felt, would be the occupation of the air, from which they had driven the Hans, and from swoopers to direct the rocket fire at the city itself. Then, when they had destroyed this, they would sweep in and hunt down the Hans, man to man, in the surrounding mountains. Command of the air was still important in military strategy, but command of the air rested no longer in the air, but on the ground.

The Hans themselves attempted to scout the American positions from the air, under cover of a massed attack of ships in "cloud bank" or beaming formation, but with very little success. Most of their ships were shot down, and the remainder slid back to the city on sharply inclined repellor rays, one of them which had its generators badly damaged while still fifty miles out, collapsed over the city, before it could reach its berth at the airport, and crashed down through the glass roof of the city, doing great damage.

Then followed the "air balls," an unforeseen and ingenious resurrection by the Americans of an old principle of air and submarine tactics, through a modern application of the principle of remote control.

The air balls took heavy toll of the morale of the Hans before they were clearly understood by them, and even afterward for that matter.

Their first appearance was quite mysterious. One uneasy night, while the pulsating growl of the distant barrage kept the nerves of the city's inhabitants on edge, there was an explosion near the top of a pinnacle not far from the Imperial Tower. It occurred at the 732nd level, and caused the structure above it to lean and sag, though it did not fall.

Repair men who shot up the shafts a few minutes later to bring new broadcast lamps to replace those which had been shattered, reported what seemed to be a sphere of metal, about three feet in diameter, with a four-inch lens in it, floating slowly down the shaft, as though it were some living creature making a careful examination, pausing now and then as its lens swung about like a great single eye. The moment this "eye" turned upon them, they said, the ball "rushed" down on them, crushing several to death in its vicious gyrations, and jamming the mechanism of the elevator, though failing to crash through it. Then, said the wounded survivors, it floated back up the shaft, watchfully "eyeing" them, and slipped off to the side at the wrecked level.

The next night several of these air balls were seen, following explosions in various towers and sections of the city roof and walls. In each case repair gangs were "rushed" by them, and suffered many casualties. On the third night a few of the air balls were destroyed by the repair men and guards, who now were equipped with disintegrator-ray pistols.

This, however, was pretty costly business, for in each case the ray bored into the corridor and shaft walls beyond its target, wrecking much machinery, injuring the structural members of that section, penetrating apartments and taking a number of lives. Moreover, the air balls, being destroyed, could not be subjected to scientific inspection.

After this the explosions ceased. But for many days the sudden appearances of those air balls in the corridors and shafts of the city caused the greatest confusion, and many times they were the cause of death and panic.

At times they released poison gases, and not infrequently themselves burst, instead of withdrawing, in a veritable explosion of disease germs, requiring absolute quarantine by the Han medical department.

There was an utter heartlessness about the defense of the Han authorities, who considered nothing but the good of the community as a whole; for when they established these quarantines, they did not hesitate to seal up thousands of the city's inhabitants behind hermetic barriers enclosing entire sections of different levels, where deprived of food and ventilation, the wretched inhabitants died miserably, long before the disease germs developed in their systems.

At the end of two weeks the entire population of the city was in a mood of panicky revolt. News service to the public had been suspended, and the use of all viewplates and phones in the city were restricted to official communications. The city administration had issued orders that all citizens not on duty should keep to their apartments, but the order was openly flouted, and small mobs were wandering through the corridors, ascending and descending from one level to another, seeking they knew not what, fleeing the air balls, which might appear anywhere, and being driven back from the innermost and deepest sections of the city by the military guard.

I now made up my mind that the time was ripe for me to attempt my escape. In all this confusion I might have an even break, in spite of the danger I might myself run from the air balls, and the almost insuperable[1] difficulties of making my way to the outside of the city and down the precipitous walls of the mountain to which the city clung like a cap. I would have given much for my inertron belt, that I might simply have leaped outward from the edge of the roof some dark night and floated gently down. I longed for my ultrophone equipment, with which I might have established communication with the beleaguering American forces.

My greatest difficulty, I knew, would be that of escaping my guard. Once free of them, I figured it would be the business of nobody in particular, in that badly disorganized city, to recapture me. The knives of the ordinary citizens I did not fear, and very few of the military guard were armed with dis-ray pistols.

I was sitting in my apartment busying my mind with various plans, when there occurred a commotion in the city corridor outside my door. The captain of my guard jumped nervously from the couch on which he had been reclining, and ordered the excited guards to open the door.

In the broad corridor, the remainder of the guard lay about, dead or groaning, where they had been bowled over by one of these air balls, the first I had ever seen.

The metal sphere floated hesitantly above its victims, turning this way and that to bring its "eye" on various objects around. It stopped dead on sighting the door the guard had thrown open, hesitated a moment, and then shot suddenly into the apartment with a hissing sound, flinging into a far corner one of the guards who had not been quick enough to duck. As the captain drew his dis-ray pistol, it launched itself at him with a vicious hiss. He bounded back from the impact, his chest crushed in, while his pistol, which fortunately had fallen with its muzzle pointed away from me, shot

---

[1] Impossible to overcome.

a continuous beam that melted its way instantly through the apartment wall.

The sphere then turned on the other guard, who had thrown himself into a corner where he crouched in fear. Deliberately it seemed to gauge the distance and direction. Then it hurled itself at him with another vicious hiss, which I now saw came from a little rocket motor, crushing him to death where he lay.

It swung slowly around until the lens faced me again, and floated gently into position level with my face, seeming to scan me with its blank, four-inch eye. Then it spoke, with a metallic voice.

"If you are an American," it said, "answer with your name, gang and position."

"I am Anthony Rogers," I replied, still half bewildered, "Boss of the Wyomings. I was captured by the Hans after my swooper was disabled in a fight with a Han airship and had drifted many hundred miles westward. These Hans you have killed were my guard."

"Good!" ejaculated the metal ball. "We have been hunting for you with these remote control rockets for two weeks. We knew you had been captured. A Han message was picked up. Close the door of your room, and hide this ball somewhere. I have turned off the rocket power. Put it on your couch. Throw some pillows over it. Get out of sight. We'll speak softly, so no Hans can hear, and we'll speak only when you speak to us."

The ball, I found, was floating freely in the air. So perfectly was it balanced with ultron and inertron that it had about the weight of a spider web. Ultimately, I suppose, it would have settled to the floor. But I had no time for such an idle experiment. I quickly pushed it to my couch, where I threw a couple of pillows and some of the bed clothes over it. Then I threw myself back on the couch with my head near it. If the dead guards outside attracted attention, and the Han patrol entered, I could report the attack by the air ball and claim that I had been knocked unconscious by it.

"One moment," said the ball, after I reported myself ready to talk. "Here is someone who wants to speak to you." And I nearly leaped from the couch with joy when, despite the metallic tone of the instrument, I recognized the eager, loving voice of my wife, almost hysterical in her own joy at talking to me again.

ESCAPE!

We had little time, however, to waste in endearments, and very little to devote to informing me as to the American plans. The essential thing was that I report the Han plans and resources to the fullest of my ability. And for an hour or two I talked steadily, giving an outline of all I had learned from San-Lan and his Councilors, and particularly of the arrangements for drawing off the population of the city to new cities concealed underground, through the system of tunnels radiating from the base of the mountain. And as a result, the Americans determined to speed up their attack.

There were, as a matter of fact, only two relatively small commands facing the city, Wilma told me, but both of them were picked troops of the new Federal Council. Those to the south were a division of veterans who a few weeks before had destroyed the Han city of Sa-Lus (St. Louis). On the east were a number of the Colorado Gangs and an expeditionary force of our own Wyomings. The attack on Lo-Tan was intended chiefly as an attack on the morale of the Hans of the other twelve cities. If there seemed to be a chance of victory, the operations were to be pushed through. Otherwise the object would be to do as much damage as possible, and fade away into the forests if the Hans developed any real pressure with their new infantry and field batteries of rocket guns and disintegrator rays.

The air balls were simply miniature swoopers of spherical shape, ultronically controlled by operators at control boards miles away, and who saw on their viewplates whatever picture the ultronic television lens in the sphere itself picked up at the predetermined focus. The main propulsive rocket motor was diametrically opposite the lens, so that the sphere could be steered simply by keeping the picture of its objective centered on the crossed hairlines of the viewplates. The outer shell moved magnetically as desired with respect to the core, which was gyroscopically stabilized. Auxiliary rocket motors enabled the operator to make a sphere move sidewise, backward, or vertically. Some of these spheres were equipped with devices which enabled their operators to hear as well as see through their ultronic broadcasts, and most of those which had invaded the interior of Lo-Tan were equipped with "speakers," in the hope of finding me and establishing communication. Still others were equipped for two-stage control. That is, the operator control led the vision sphere, and through it watched and steered an air torpedo that traveled ahead of it.

The Han airship or any other target selected by the operator of such a combination was doomed. There was no escape. The spheres and torpedoes were too small to be hit. They could travel with the speed of bullets. They could trail a ship indefinitely, hover a safe distance from their mark, and strike at will. Finally, neither darkness nor smoke screens were any bar to their ultronic vision. The spheres, which had penetrated and explored Lo-Tan in their search for me, had floated through breaches in the walls and roofs made by their advance torpedoes.

Wilma had just finished explaining all this to me when I heard a noise outside my door. With a whispered warning I flung myself back on the couch and simulated unconsciousness. When I did not answer the poundings and calls to open, a police detail broke in and shook me roughly.

"The air ball," I moaned, pretending to regain consciousness slowly. "It came in from the corridor. Look what it did to the guard. It must have grazed my head. Where is it?"

"Gone," muttered the under-officer, looking fearfully around. "Yes, undoubtedly gone. These men have been dead some time. And this pistol. The ball got him before he had a chance to use it. See, it has beamed through the wall only here, where he dropped it. Who are you? You look like a tribesman. Oh, yes, you're the Heaven-Born's special prisoner. Maybe I ought to beam you right now. Good thing. Everyone would call it an accident. By the Grand Dragon, I will!"

While he was talking, I had staggered to the other side of the room, to draw his attention away from the couch where the ball was concealed.

Now suddenly the pillows burst apart, and a blanket with which I had covered the thing streaked from the couch, hitting the man in the small of the back. I could hear his spine snap under the impact. Then it shot through the air toward the group of soldiers in the doorway, bowling them over and sending them shrieking right and left along the corridor. Relentlessly and with amazing speed it launched itself at each in turn, until the corpses lay grotesquely strewn about, and not one had escaped.

It returned to me for all the world like an old-fashioned ghost, the blanket still draped over it (and not interfering with its ultronic vision in the least) and "stood" before me.

"The yellow devils were going to kill you, Tony," I heard Wilma's voice saying. "You've got to get out of there, Tony, before you are killed. Besides, we need you at the control boards, where you can make real use of your knowledge of the city. Have you your jumping belt, ultrophone, and rocket gun?"

"No," I replied, "they are all gone."

"It would be no good for you to try to make your way to one of the breaches in the wall, nor to the roof," she mused.

"No, they are too well guarded," I replied, "and even if you made

ch. ends p. 170

a new one at a predetermined spot I'm afraid the repair men and the patrol would go to it ahead of me."

"Yes, and they would beam you before you could climb inside of a swooper," she added.

"I'll tell you what I can do, Wilma," I suggested. "I know my way about the city pretty well. Suppose I go down one of the shafts to the base of the mountain. I think I can get out. It is dark in the valley, so the Hans cannot see me, and I will stand out in the open, where your ultroscopes can pick me up. Then a swooper can drop quickly down and get me."

"Good!" Wilma said. "But take that Han's dis-ray pistol with you. And go right away, Tony. But wrap this ball in something and carry it with you. Just toss it from you if you are attacked. I'll stay at the control board and operate it in case of emergency."

So I picked up ball and pistol, and thrust the hand in which I held it into the loose Han blouse I wore, wrapped the ball in a piece of sheeting, and stepped out in the corridor, hurrying toward the nearest magnetic car station, a couple of hundred feet down the corridor, for I had to cross nearly the entire width of the city to reach the shaft that went to the base of the mountain.

I thanked Providence for the perfection of the Han mechanical devices when I reached the station. The automatic checking system of these cars made station attendants unnecessary. I had only to slip the key I had taken from the dead Han officer into the account-charting machine at the station to release a car.

Pressing the proper combinations of main and branch line buttons, I seated myself, holding the pistol ready but concealed beneath my blouse. The car shot with rapid acceleration down the narrow tunnel.

The tubes in which these magnetic cars (which slid along a few inches above the floor of the tunnel by localized repellor rays) ran were very narrow, just the width of the car, and my only danger would come if on catching up to another car its driver should turn around and look in my face. If I kept my face to the front, and hunched over so as to conceal my size, no driver of a following car would suspect that I was not a Han like himself.

The tube dipped under traffic as it came to a trunk line, and my car magnetically lagged, until an opening in the traffic permitted it to swing swiftly into the main line tunnel. At the automatic distance of ten feet it followed a car in which rode a scantily clad girl, her flimsy silks fluttering in the rush of air. I cursed my luck. She would be far more likely to turn around than a man, to see if a man were in the car behind, and if he were personable—for not even the impending doom of the city and the public demoralization caused by the air balls had dulled the proclivities of the Han women for brazen flirtation. And turn around she did.

Before I could lower my head she had seen my face, and knew I was no Han. I saw her eyebrows arch in surprise. But she seemed puzzled rather than scared. Before she could make up her mind about me, however, her car had swung out of the main tunnel on its predetermined course, and my own automatically was closing up the gap to the car ahead. The passenger in this one wore the uniform of a medical officer, but he did not turn around before I swung out of main traffic to the little station at the head of the shaft.

This particular shaft was intended to serve the very lowest levels exclusively, and since its single car carried nothing but express traffic, it was used only by repair men and other specialists who occasionally had to descend to those levels.

There were only three people on the little platform, which reminded me very much of the subway stations of the 20th century. Two men and a girl stood facing the gate of the shaft, waiting for the car to return from below. One of these was a soldier, apparently off duty, for though he wore the scarlet military coat he carried no weapons other than his knife. The other man wore nothing but sandals and a pair of loose short pants of some heavy and serviceable

ch. ends p. 170

material. I did not need to look at the compact tool kit and the ray machines attached to his heavy belt, nor the gorgeously jeweled armlet and diadem[1] that he wore to know him for a repair man.

The girl was quite scantily clad, but wore a mask, which was not unusual among the Han women when they went forth on their flirtatious expeditions, and there was something about the sinuous grace of her movements that seemed familiar to me. She was making desperate love to the repair man, whose attitude toward her was that of pleased but lofty tolerance. The soldier, who was seeking no trouble, occupied himself strictly with his own thoughts and paid little attention to them.

I stepped from my car, still carrying my bundle in which the air ball was concealed, and the car shot away as I threw the release lever over. Not so successful as the soldier in simulating lack of interest in the amorous girl and her companion, I drew from the latter a stare of haughty challenge, and the girl herself turned to look at me through her mask.

She gasped as she did so, and shrank back in alarm. And I knew her then in spite of her mask. She was the favorite of the Heaven-Born himself.

"Ngo-Lan!" I exclaimed before I could catch myself.

At the mention of her name, the soldier's head jerked up quickly, and the girl herself gave a little cry of terror, shrinking against her burly companion. This would mean death for her if it reached the ears of her lord.

And her companion, arrogant in his immunity as a repair man, hesitated not a second. His arm shot out toward the soldier, who was nearer to him than I. There was the flash of a knife blade, and the soldier sagged on his feet, then tumbled over like a sack of potatoes, and before my mind had grasped the danger, he had swept the girl aside and was springing at me.

That I lived for a moment even was due to the devotion of my wife, Wilma, who somewhere in the mountains to the east was standing loyally before the control board of the air ball I carried.

For even as the Han leaped at me, the bundle containing the air ball, which I had placed at my feet, shot diagonally upward,

---

[1] An ornamental headband worn as a symbol of royalty.

catching the fellow in the middle of his leap, hurling him back against the grilled gate of the elevator shaft, and pinning his lifeless body there.

An instant the girl gazed in speechless horror at what had been her secret lover, then she threw herself at my feet, writhing and shrieking in terror.

At this moment, the elevator shot to a sudden stop behind the grill, and prepared for the worst, I faced it, dis-ray pistol raised.

But I lowered the pistol at once, with a sigh of relief. The elevator was empty. For a moment I considered. I dared not leave either of these bodies nor the girl behind in descending the shaft. At any moment other passengers might glide out of the tunnel to take the elevator, and give an alarm.

So I played the beam of the pistol for an instant on the two dead bodies. They vanished, of course, into nothingness, as did part of the station platform. The damage to the platform, however, would not necessarily be interpreted as evidence of a prisoner escaping.

Then I threw open the elevator gate, dragging Ngo-Lan into the car and stifling her hysterical shrieks, pressed the button that caused it to shoot downward. In a few moments I stepped out several thousand feet below, into a shaft that ran toward one of the Valley Gates.

The pistol again became serviceable, this time for the destruction of the elevator, thus blocking any possible pursuit, yet without revealing my flight.

Ngo-Lan fought like a cat, but despite her writhing, scratching and biting, I bound and gagged her with her own clothing, and left her lying in the tunnel while I stepped in a car and shot toward the gate.

As the car glided swiftly along the brilliantly lit but deserted tunnel I conversed again with Wilma through the metallic speaker of the air ball.

"The only obstacle now," I told her, "is the massive gate at the end of the tunnel. The gate-guard, I think, is posted both outside and inside the gate."

"In that case, Tony," she replied, "I will shoot the ball ahead, and blow out the gate. When you hear it bump against the gate, throw

ch. ends next p.

yourself flat in the car, for an instant later I will explode it. Then you can rush through the gate into the night. Scoutships are now hovering above, and they will see you with their ultroscopes, though the darkness will leave you invisible to the Hans."

With this the ball shot out of the car and flashed away, down the tunnel ahead of me. I heard a distant metallic thump, and crouched low in the speeding car, clapping my hands to my ears. The heavy detonation which followed, struck me like a blow, and left me gasping for breath. The car staggered like a living thing that had been struck, then gathered speed again and shot forward toward the gaping black hole where the gate had been.

I brought it to a stop at the pile of debris, and climbed through this to freedom and the night. Stumblingly, I made my way out into the open and waited.

Behind, and far above me on the mountain peak, the lights of the city gleamed and flashed, while the iridescent beams of countless disintegrator ray batteries on surrounding mountain peaks played continuously and nervously, criss-crossing in the sky above it.

Then with a swish, a line dropped out of the sky, and a little seat rested on the ground beside me. I climbed into it, and without further ado was whisked up into the swooper that floated a few hundred feet above me.

A half an hour later I was deposited in a little forest glade where the headquarters of the Wyoming Gang were located, and was greeted with a frantic disregard for decorum by the Deputy Boss of the Wyomings, who rushed upon me like a whirlwind, laughing, crying, and whispering endearments all in the same breath, while I squeezed her, Wilma, my wife, until at last she gasped for mercy.

14

THE DESTRUCTION OF LO-TAN

"How did you know I had been taken to Lo-Tan as a prisoner?"
I asked the little group of Wyoming Bosses who had assembled in
Wilma's tent to greet me. "And how does it happen that our gang is
away out here in the Rocky Mountains? I had expected, after the
fall of Nu-Yok, that you would join the forest ring around Bah-Flo
(Buffalo I called it in the 20th century) or the forces beleaguering
Bos-Tan."

They explained that my encounter with the Han airship had
been followed carefully by several scopemen. They had seen my
swooper shoot skyward out of control, and had followed it with
their telultronoscopes until it had been caught in a gale at a high
level, and wafted swiftly westward. Ultronophone warnings had
been broadcast, asking western Gangs to rescue me if possible. Few
of the Gangs west of the Alleghanies, however, had any swoopers,
and though I was frequently reported, no attempts could be made to
rescue me. Scopemen had reported my capture by the Han ground
post, and my probable incarceration in Lo-Tan.

The Rocky Mountain Gangs, in planning their campaign against
Lo-Tan, had appealed to the east for help, and Wilma had led the

Wyoming veterans westward, though the other eastern Gang had divided their aid between the armies before Bah-Flo and Bos-Tan.

The heavy bombardment which I had heard from Lo-Tan, they told me, was merely a test of the enemy's tactics and strength, but it accomplished little other than to develop that the Hans had the mountains and peaks thickly planted with rocket gunners of their own. It was almost impossible to locate these gun posts, for they were well camouflaged from air observation, and widely scattered; nor did they reveal their positions when they went into action as did their ray batteries.

The Hans apparently were abandoning their rays except for air defense. I told what I knew of the Han plans for abandoning the city, and their escape tunnels. On the strength of this, a general council of Gang Bosses was called. This council agreed that immediate action was necessary, for my escape from the city probably would be suspected, and San-Lan would be inclined to start an exodus at once.

As a matter of fact, the destruction of the city presented no real problem to us at all. Explosive air balls could be sent against any target under a control that could not be better were their operators riding within them, and with no risk to the operators. When a ball was exploded on its target by the operator, or destroyed by accident, he simply reported the fact to the supply division, and a fresh one was placed on the jump-off, tuned to his controls.

To my own Gang, the Wyomings, the Council delegated the destruction of the escape tunnels of the enemy. We had a comfortably located camp in a wooded canyon, some hundred and thirty miles northeast of the city, with about 500 men, most of whom were bayonet-gunners, 350 girls as long-gunners and control-board operators, 91 control boards and about 250 five-foot, inertron-protected air balls, of which 200 were of the explosive variety.

I ordered all control boards manned, taking Number One myself, and instructed the others to follow my lead in single file, at the minimum interval of safety, with their projectiles set for signal rather than contact detonation.

In my mind I paid humble tribute to the ingenuity of our engineers as I gently twisted the lever that shot my projectile vertically into the air from the jump-off clearing some half mile away.

The control board before me was a compact contrivance about five feet square. The center of it contained a four-foot viewplate. Whatever view was picked up by the ultronoscope "eye" of the air ball was automatically broadcast on an accurate tuning channel to this viewplate by the automatic mechanism of the projectile. In turn my control board broadcast the signals which automatically controlled the movements of the ball.

Above and below the viewplate were the pointers and the swinging needles which indicated the speed and angle of vertical movement, the altimeter, the directional compass, and the horizontal speed and distance indicators.

At my left hand was the lever by which I could set the "eye" for penetrative, normal, or varying degrees of telescopic vision, and at my right the universally jointed stick (much like the "joy stick" of the ancient airplanes) with its speed control button on the top, with which the ball was directionally "pointed" and controlled.

The manipulation of these levers I had found, with a very little practice, most instinctive and simple.

So, as I have said, I pointed my projectile straight up and let it shoot to the height of two miles. Then I leveled it off, and shot it at full speed (about 500 miles an hour with no allowance for air currents) in a general southwesterly direction, while I eased my controls until I brought in the telescopic view of Lo-Tan. I centered the picture of the city on the crossed hairlines in the middle of my viewpoint, and watched its image grow.

In about fifteen minutes the "string" of air balls was before the city, and speaking in my ultrophone I gave the order to halt, while I swung the scope control to the penetrative setting and let my "eye"

ch. ends p. 177

rove slowly back and forth through the walls of the city, hunting for a spot from which I might get my bearings. At last, after many penetrations, I managed to bring in a view of the head of the shaft at the bottom of which I knew the tunnels were located, and saw that we were none too soon, for all the corridors leading toward this shaft were packed with Hans waiting their turn to descend.

Slowly I let my "eye" retreat down one of these corridors until I "pulled it out" through the outer wall of the city. There I held the spot on the crossed hairlines and ordered Number Two Operator to my control board, where I pointed out to her the exact spot where I desired a breach in the wall. Returning to her own board, she withdrew her ball from the "string," and focusing on this spot in the wall, eased her projectile into contact with it and detonated.

The atomic force of the explosion shattered a vast section of the wall, and for the moment I feared I had balked my own game by not having provided a less powerful projectile.

After some fumbling, however, I was able to maneuver my ball through a gap in the debris and find the corridor I was seeking. Down this corridor I sent it at the speed of a 20th century bullet, (this is to say, about half speed) to spare myself the sight of the slaughter as it cut a swath down the closely packed column of the enemy. If there were any it did not kill, I knew they would be taken care of by the other balls in the string which would follow.

I had to slow it up, however, near the head of the shaft to take my bearings; and a sea of evil faces, contorted with livid terror, looked at me from my viewplate. But not even the terror could conceal the hate in those faces, and there arose in my mind the picture of their long centuries of ruthless cruelty to my race, and the hopelessness of changing the tigerish nature of these Hans. So I steeled myself, and drove the ball again and again into that sea of faces, until I had cleared the station platform of any living enemy, and sent the survivors crushing their way madly along the corridors away from it. There was blinding flash or two on my viewplate as some Han officer tried his dis-ray pistol on my projectile, but that was all, except that he must have disintegrated many of his fellows, for our balls were sheathed in inertron, and suffered no damage themselves.

Cautioning my unit to follow carefully, I pushed my control

lever all the way forward until my "eye" pointed down, and there appeared on my viewplate the smooth cylindrical interior of the shaft, fading down toward the base of the mountain, and like a tiny speck, far, far down, was the car, descending with its last load.

I dropped my ball on it, battering it down to the bottom of the shaft, and with hammer-like blows flattening the wreckage, that I might squeeze the ball out of the shaft at the lower station.

It emerged into the great vaulted excavation, capable of holding a thousand or more persons, from which the various escape tunnels radiated. Down these tunnels the last remnants of a crowd of fugitives were disappearing, while red-coated soldiers guided the traffic and suppressed disorder with the threat of their spears, and the occasional flourish of a dis-ray pistol.

As I floated my ball out into the middle of the artificial cavern I could see them stagger back in terror. Again the blinding flashes of a few pistols, and instantaneous borings of the rays into the walls. The red coats nearest the escape tunnels fled down them in panic. Those whose escape I blocked dropped their weapons and shrank back against the smooth, iridescent green walls.

I marshaled the rest of my string carefully into the cavern, and counted the tunnel entrances, slowly swinging my "eye" around the semicircle of them. There were 26 corridors diverging to the north and west. I decided to send three balls down each, leave 12 in the cavern, then detonate them all at once.

Assigning my operators to their corridors, I ordered intervals of five miles between them, and taking the lead down the first corridor, I ordered "go."

Soon my ball overtook the stream of fugitives, smashing them down despite dis-ray pistols and even rockets that were shot against it. On and on I drove it, time and again battering it through detachments of fleeing Hans, while the distance register on my board climbed to ten, twenty, fifty miles.

Then I called a halt, and suspended my previous orders. I had had no idea that the Hans had bored these tunnels for such distances under the surface of the ground as this. It would be necessary to trace them to their ends and locate their new underground cities in which they expected to establish themselves, and in which many had established themselves by now, no doubt.

Fifty miles of air in these corridors, I thought, ought to prove a pretty good cushion against the shock of detonation in the cavern. So I ordered detonation of the twelve balls we had left behind. As I expected, there was little effect from it so far out in the tunnels.

But from our scopemen who were covering the city from the outside, I learned that the effects of the explosion on the mountain were terrific; far more than I had dared to hope for.

The mountain itself burst asunder in several spots, throwing out thousands of tons of earth and rock. One-half the city itself tore loose and slid downward, lost in the debris of the avalanche of which it was a part. The remainder, wrenched and convulsed like a living thing in agony, cracked, crumbled and split, towers tumbling down and great fissures appearing in its walls. Its power plant and electro machinery went out of commission. Fifteen of its scoutships hovering in the air directly above, robbed of the power broadcast and their repellor beams disappearing, crashed down into the ruins.

But out in the escape tunnels, we continued our explorations, now sure that no warnings could be broadcast to the tunnel exits, and mowed down contingent after contingent of the hated yellow men.

My register showed seventy-five miles before I came to the end of the tunnel, and drove my ball out into a vast underground city of great, brilliantly illuminated corridors, some of them hundreds of feet high and wide. The architectural scheme was one of lace-like structures of curving lines and of indescribable beauty.

Word had reached us now of the destruction of the city itself, so that no necessity existed for destroying the escape tunnels. In consequence, I ordered the two operators, who were following me, to send their balls out into this underground city, seeking the shaft which the Hans were sure to have as a secret exit to the surface of the earth above.

But at this juncture events of transcending importance inter-rupted my plans for a thorough exploration of these new subter-ranean cities of the Hans. I detonated my projectile at once and ordered all of the operators to do so, and to tune in instantly on new ones. That we wrecked most of these new cities I now know, but of course at the time we were in the dark as to how much damage we caused, since our viewplates naturally went dead when we detonated our projectiles.

15

THE COUNTER-ATTACK

The news which caused me to change my plans was grave enough. As I have explained, the American lines lay roughly to the east and the south of the city in the mountains. My own Gang held the northern flank of the east line. To the south of us was the Colorado Union, a force of 5,000 men and about 2,000 girls recruited from about fifteen Gangs. They were a splendid organization, well disciplined and equipped. Their posts, rather widely distributed, occupied the mountain tops and other points of advantage to a distance of about a hundred and fifty miles to the south. There the line turned east, and was held by the Gangs which had come up from the south. Now, simultaneously with the reports from my scouts that a large Han land force was working its way down on us from the north, and threatening to outflank us, came word from Jim Hallwell, Big Boss of the Colorado Union and the commander in chief of our army, that another large Han force was to the southwest of our western flank. And in addition, it seemed, most of the Han military forces at Lo-Tan had been moved out of the city and advanced toward our lines before our air-ball attack.

The situation would not have been in the least alarming if the Hans had had no better arms to fight with than their disintegrator rays, which naturally revealed the locations of their generators the second the visible beams went into play, and their airships, which we had learned how to bring down, first from the air, and now from the ground, through ultrono-controlled projectiles.

But the Hans had learned their lesson from us by this time. Their electrono-chemists had devised atomic projectiles, rocket-propelled, very much like our own, which could be launched in a terrific barrage without revealing the locations of their batteries, and they had equipped their infantry with rocket guns not dissimilar to ours. This division of their army had been expanded by general conscription.[1] So far as ordnance was concerned, we had little advantage over them; although tactically we were still far superior, for our jumping belts enabled our men and girls to scale otherwise inaccessible heights, conceal themselves readily in the upper branches of the giant trees, and gave them a general all around mobility, the enemy could not hope to equal.

We had the advantage too, in our ultronophones and scopes, in a field of energy which the Hans could not penetrate, while we could cut in on their electrono or (as I would have called it in the 20th century) radio broadcasts.

Later reports showed that there were no less than 10,000 Hans in the force to our north, which evidently was equipped with a portable power broadcast, sufficient for communication purposes and the local operation of small scoutships, painted a green which made them difficult to distinguish against the mountain and forest backgrounds. These ships just skimmed the surface of the terrain, hardly ever outlining themselves against the sky. Moreover, the Han commanders wisely had refrained from massing their forces. They had developed over a very wide and deep front, in small units, well scattered, which were driving down the parallel valleys and canyons like spearheads. Their communications were

---

[1] Compulsory enrollment of persons for military or naval service; draft.

working well too, for our scouts reported their advance as well restrained, and maintaining a perfect front as between valley and valley, with a secondary line of heavy batteries, moved by small airships from peak to peak, following along the ridges somewhat behind the valley forces.

Hallwell had determined to withdraw our southern wing, pivoting it back to face the outflanking Han force on that side, which had already worked its way well down in back of our line.

In the ultronophone council which we held at once, each Boss tuning in on Hallwell's band, though remaining with his unit, Wilma and I pleaded for a vigorous attack rather than a defensive maneuver. Our suggestion was to divide the American forces into three divisions, with all the swoopers forming a special reserve, and to advance with a rush on the three Han forces behind a rolling barrage.

But the best we could do was to secure permission to make such an attack with our Wyomings, if we wished, to serve as a diversion while the lines were reforming. And two of the southern Gangs on the west flank, which were eager to get at the enemy, received the same permission.

The rest of the army fumed at the caution of the council, but it spoke well for their discipline that they did not take things in their own hands, for in the eyes of those forest men who had been hounded for centuries, the chance to spring at the throats of the Hans outweighed all other considerations.

So, as the council signed off, Wilma and I turned to the eager faces that surrounded us, and issued our orders.

In a moment the air was filled with leaping figures as the men and girls shot away over the treetops and up the mountain sides in the deployment movement.

A group of our engineers threw themselves headlong toward a cave across the valley, where they had rigged out a powerful electrono plant operating from atomic energy. And a few moments

ch. ends next p.

later the little portable receiver, the Intelligence Boss used to pick up the enemy messages, began to emit such ear-splitting squeals and howls that he shut it off. Our heterodyne or "radio-scrambling" broadcast had gone into operation, emitting impulses of constantly varying wavelength over the full broadcast range and heterodyning the Han communications into futility.

In a little while our scouts came leaping down the valley from the north, and our air balls now were hovering above the Han lines, operators at the control boards nearby painstakingly picking up the pictures of the Han squads struggling down the valleys with their comparatively clumsy weapons.

As fast as the air-ball scopes picked out these squads, their operators, each of whom was in ultronophone communication with a girl long-gunner at some spot in our line, would inform her of the location of the enemy unit, and the latter, after a bit of mathematical calculation, would send a rocket into the air which would come roaring down on, or very near that unit, and wipe it out.

But for all of that, the number of the Han squads were too much for us. And for every squad we destroyed, fifty advanced.

And though the lines were still several miles apart, in most places, and in some cases with mountain ridges intervening, the Han fire control began to sense the general location of our posts, and things became more serious as their rockets too began to hiss down and explode here and there in our lines, not infrequently killing or maiming one or more of our girls.

The men, our bayonet-gunners, had not as yet suffered, for they were well in advance of the girls, under strict orders to shoot no rockets nor in any way reveal their positions; so the Han rockets were going over their heads.

The Hans in the valleys now were shooting diagonal barrages up the slopes toward the ridges, where they suspected we would be most strongly posted, thus making a crossfire up the two sides of a ridge, while their heavy batteries, somewhat in the rear, shot straight along the tops of the ridges. But their valley forces were getting out of alignment a bit by now, owing to our heterodyne operations.

I ordered our swoopers, of which we had five, to sweep along above these ridges and destroy the Han batteries.

Up in the higher levels where they were located, the Hans had little cover. A few of their small rep-ray ships rose to meet our swoopers, but were battered down. One swooper they brought to earth with a disintegrator ray beam, by creating a vacuum beneath it, but they did it no serious damage, for its fall was a light one. Subsequently it did tremendous damage, cleaning off an entire ridge.

Another swooper ran into a catastrophe that had one chance in a million of occurring. It hit a heavy Han rocket nose to nose. Inertron sheathing and all, it was blown into powder.

But the others accomplished their jobs excellently. Small, two-man ships, streaking straight at the Hans at between 600 and 700 miles an hour, they could not be hit except by sheer amazing luck, and they showered their tiny but powerful bombs everywhere as they went.

At the same instant I ordered the girls to cease sharpshooting and lay their barrages down in the valleys, with their long-guns set for maximum automatic advance, and to feed the reservoirs as fast as possible, while the bayonet-gunners leaped along close behind this barrage.

Then, with a 20th century urge to see with my own eyes rather than through a viewplate, and to take part in the action, I turned command over to Wilma and leaped away, fifty feet a jump, up the valley, toward the distant flashes and rolling thunder.

VICTORY

I had gone five miles and paused for a moment, halfway up the slope of the valley to get my bearings, when a figure came hurtling through the air from behind and landed lightly at my side. It was Wilma.

"I put Bill Hearn in command and followed, Tony. I won't let you go into that alone. If you die, I do, too. Now don't argue, dear. I'm determined."

So together we leaped northward again toward the battle. And after a bit we pulled up close behind the barrage.

Great, blinding flashes, like a continuous wall of gigantic fireworks, receded up the valley ahead of us, sweeping ahead of it a seething, tossing mass of debris that seemed composed of all nature, tons of earth, rocks and trees. Ever and anon[1] vast sections of the mountain sides would loosen and slide into the valley.

And, leaping close behind this barrage, with a reckless skill and courage that amazed me, our bayonet-gunners appeared in a continuous series of flashing pictures, outlined in midleap against the wall of fire.

I would not have believed it possible for such a barrage to

[1] Soon; shortly.

pass over any of the enemy and leave them unscathed. But it did. For the Hans, operating small disintegrator beams from local or field broadcasts, frantically bored deep, slanting holes in the earth as the fiery tides of explosions rolled up the valleys toward them, and into these probably half of their units were able to throw themselves and escape destruction.

But dazed and staggering they came forth again only to meet death from the terrible, ripping, slashing, cleaving weapons in the hands of our leaping bayonet-gunners.

Thrust! Cut! Crunch! Slice! Thrust! Up and down with vicious, tireless, flashing speed, swung the bayonets and ax-bladed butts of the American gunners as they leaped and dodged, ever forward, toward new opponents.

Weakly and ineffectually the red-coated Han soldiery thrust at them with spears, flailing with their short swords and knives, or whipping about their dis-ray pistols. The forest men were too powerful, too fast in their remorselessly efficient movement.

With a shout of unholy joy, I gripped a bayonet-gun from the hands of a gunner whose leg had been whisked out of existence beneath him by a pistol ray, and leaped forward into the fight, launching myself at a red-coated officer who was just stepping out of a "wormhole."

Like a shriek of the Valkyrie, Wilma's battle cry rang in my ear as she, too, shot herself like a rocket at a red-coated figure.

I thrust with every ounce of my strength. The Han officer, grinning wickedly as he tried to raise the muzzle of his pistol, threw himself backward as my bayonet ripped the air under his nose. But his grin turned instantly to sickened surprise as the up-cleaving ax-blade on the butt of my weapon caught him in the groin, half bisecting him.

And from the corner of my eye I saw Wilma bury her bayonet in her opponent, screaming in ecstatic joy.

And so, in a matter of seconds, we found ourselves in the front rank, thrusting, cutting, dodging, leaping along behind that blinding and deafening barrage in a veritable whirlwind of fury, until it seemed to me that we were exulting in a consciousness of excelling even that tide of destruction in our merciless efficiency.

At last we became aware, in but a vague sort of way at first, that no more red-coats were rising up out of the ground to go down again before our whirling, swinging weapons. Gradually we paused, looking about in wonder. Then the barrage ceased, and the sudden absence of the deafening roll, and the wall of light, in themselves, deafened and blinded us.

I leaped weakly toward the spot where hazily I spied Wilma, now drooping and swaying on her feet, supported as she was by her jumping belt, and caught her in my arms, just as she was sinking gently to the ground.

All around us the weary warriors, crimsoned now with the blood of the enemy, were sinking to the ground in exhaustion. And as I too, sank down, clutching in my arms the unconscious form of my warrior wife, I began to hear, through my helmet phones, the exultant report of headquarters.

Our attack had swept straight through the enemy's sector, completely annihilating everything except a few hundred of his troops on either flank. And these, in panic and terror, had scattered wildly in flight. We had wiped out a force more than ten times our own number. The right flank of the American army was saved. And already the Colorado Union, from behind us, was leaping around in a great circling movement, closing in on the Han force that was advancing from the ruins of Lo-Tan.

Far away, to the southwest, the southern Gangs, reinforced in the end by the bulk of our left wing, had struck straight at the enveloping Han force shattering it like a thunderbolt, and at present were busily hunting down and destroying its scattered remnants.

But before the Colorado Union could complete the destruction of the central division of the enemy, the despairing Hans saved them the trouble. Company after company of them, knowing no escape was possible, lined up in the forest glades and valleys, while their officers swept them out of existence by the hundreds with their dis-ray pistols, which they then turned on themselves.

And so the fall of Lo-Tan was accomplished. Somewhere in the seething activities of these few days, San-Lan, the "Heaven-Born," Emperor of the Hans in America, perished, for he was heard of never again, and the unified action of the Hans vanished with him,

ch. ends p. 190

though it was several years before one by one their remaining cities were destroyed and their populations hunted down, thus completing the reclamation of America and inaugurating the most glorious and noble era of scientific civilization in the history of the American race.

As I look back on those emotional and violent years from my present vantage point of declining existence in an age of peace and good will toward all mankind, they do seem savage and repellent.

Then there flashes into my memory the picture of Wilma (now long since gone to her rest) as, screaming in an utter abandon of merciless fury, she threw herself recklessly, exultantly into the thick of that wild, relentless slaughter; and my mind can find nothing savage nor repellent about her.

If I, product of the relatively peaceful 20th century, was so completely carried away by the fury of that war, intensified by centuries of unspeakable cruelty on the part of the yellow men who were mentally gods and morally beasts, shall I be shocked at the "bloodthirstiness" of a mate who was, after all, but a normal girl of that day, and who, girl as she was, never for a moment faltered in the high courage with which she threw herself into that combat, responding to the passionate urge for freedom in her blood that not five centuries of inhuman persecution could subdue?

Had the Hans been raging tigers, or slimy, loathsome reptiles, would we have spared them? And when in their centuries of degradation they had destroyed the souls within themselves, were they in any way superior to tigers or snakes? To have extended mercy would have been suicide.

In the years that followed, Wilma and I traveled nearly every nation on the earth which had succeeded in throwing off the Han domination, spurred on by our success in America, and I never knew her to show to the men or women of any race anything but the utmost of sympathetic courtesy and consideration, whether they were the noble brown-skinned Caucasians of India, the sturdy

Balkanites of Southern Europe, or the simple, spiritual Blacks of Africa, today one of the leading races of the world, although in the 20th century we regarded them as inferior. This charity and gentleness of hers did not fail even in our contacts with the non-Han Mongolians of Japan and the coast provinces of China.

But that monstrosity among the races of men which originated as a hybrid somewhere in the dark fastnesses of interior Asia, and spread itself like an inhuman yellow blight over the face of the globe—for that race, like all of us, she felt nothing but horror and the irresistible urge to extermination.

Latterly, our historians and anthropologists find much support for the theory that the Hans sprang from a genus of human-like creatures that may have arrived on this earth with a small planet (or large meteor) which is known to have crashed in interior Asia late in the 20th century, causing certain permanent changes in the earth's orbit and climate.

Geological convulsions blocked this section off from the rest of the world for many years. And it is a historical fact that Chinese scientists, driving their explorations into it at a somewhat later period, met the first wave of the on-coming Hans.

The theory is that these creatures (and certain queer skeletons have been found in the "Asiatic Bowl") with a mental superdevelopment, but a vacuum in place of that intangible something we call a soul, mated forcibly with the Tibetans, thereby strengthening their physical structure to almost the human normal, adapting themselves to earthly speech and habits, and in some strange manner intensifying even further their mental powers.

Or, to put it the other way around. These Tibetans, through the injection of this unearthly blood, deteriorated slightly physically, lost the "soul" parts of their nature entirely, and developed abnormally efficient intellects.

However, through the centuries that followed, as the Hans spread over the face of the earth, this unearthly strain in them not

ch. ends next p.

only became more dilute, but lost its potency; and in the end, the poison of it submerged the power of it, and earth's mankind came again into possession of its inheritance.

How all this may be, I do not know. It is merely a hypothesis over which the learned men of today quarrel.

But I do know that there was something inhuman about these Hans. And I had many months of intimate contact with them, and with their Emperor in America. I can vouch for the fact that even in his most friendly and human moments, there was an inhumanity, or perhaps "unhumanity" about him that aroused in me that urge to kill.

But whether or not there was in these people blood from outside this planet, the fact remains that they have been exterminated, that a truly human civilization reigns once more—and that I am now a very tired old man, waiting with no regrets for the call which will take me to another existence.

There, it is my hope and my conviction that my courageous mate of those bloody days waits for me with loving arms.

AFTERWORD

Of all the stories selected for reprinting by *Amazing Stories*, none have received the acclamation of *Armageddon 2419 A.D.*, the first Buck Rogers story published in the April 1961, 35th Anniversary issue. Readers were amazed by the terse writing, the superb knowledge of military tactics, the brilliant prophecies of rocket guns, walkie talkies, jet planes, infrared ray sights, and many other devices which have become part and parcel of modern warfare.

The Airlords of Han, sequel to *Armageddon 2419 A.D.*, is in every meaning of the phrase a command performance for readers of *Amazing Stories*. While many other stories may have received greater publicity through the years, and other authors achieved more meaningful fame, Philip Francis Nowlan's work has not been unknown to prime movers in the field. At the time of Nowlan's sudden death from a stroke in 1940, John W. Campbell, Jr., who read the Buck Rogers stories when they first appeared and was at that very time scheduling the last story the man was ever to write, said: "The quality of Nowlan's written science fiction was certainly exceptionally high—even ten years ago, when the magazine science fiction was only starting, the work Phil Nowlan did was of a grade that would have been acceptable and well rated against the much more highly evolved work of today. He had, then, developed one of the concepts that has only recently been generally recognized and used: the realization that the thought-patterns of the people of the future will necessarily be as different from the everyday thought-matrices of our present as their background must differ from ours."

The Airlords of Han will prove a delight to the readers. Hugo Gernsback when "blurbing" it in 1929 said: "Mr. Nowlan has quite outdone himself. In our humble opinion, the sequel is in many respects better than the original story." That statement is, in my opinion, true. This is a marvelous story from many standpoints.

First of all from the aspect of the storytellers art, it is told with a directness, precise imagery, and discipline of controlled imagination that has relatively limited competition among science fiction authors living or dead. The obvious grasp of military tactics, so strikingly evidenced in the first story, is reaffirmed here.

Here, too, the sound basis of the scientific prophecy has few equals. The war of the future is fought *with rockets that sport atomic warheads!* No indirection in prophecy. No broad gesture that could be interpreted as the foregoing, but the very terms spelled out for the very purpose we use them today *and this is a story printed in 1929,* not one appearing in 1944 or 1945, when the events were nearly upon us.

Buttressing the inventions are the sound, military reasons for their use and their limitations. You will find that the United States initially was devastated after a war with the Bolsheviks. You will stand back aghast as psychoanalysts (called that) practice brainwashing for political and military reasons. Public television for personal communication, like the telephone (recently instituted to a limited degree in Russia) is standard practice. Germ warfare is effectively practiced. Radio controlled rocket powered television scanners send back picture and words to the operator, not unlike what some of our earth satellites are doing today.

All of this is placed logically in a society whose social system, business structure, and mores are carefully, integrated with the scientific material.

It was no accident that Buck Rogers became an almost instantaneous success as a comic strip. Behind its creation was one of the most logical, scientifically planned "worlds of if" ever conceived. The re-presentation of these original Buck Rogers stories secures for Philip Francis Nowlan the important place he deserves as a shaper of modern science fiction.

Sam Moskowitz
Amazing Stories
May 1962

Philip Francis Nowlan

AMERICAN RADIOACTIVE
Gas Corporation

Wyoming, Pennsylvania

Printed in the USA
CPSIA information can be obtained
at www.ICGtesting.com
JSHW022346101123
51467JS00006B/110

9 781948 316163